Brad?

Samantha started up at the man in shock.
She'd seen him just eight months ago, but he
looked...different. Incredibly different. His glasses
were gone, he wore a dark gray, pin-striped suit
that looked tailor-made, and silver cuff links.

But the difference went beyond clothes. He
smelled of expensive gabardine, fine linen
and spicy cologne. He was still tall and lean,
but his shoulders looked broader. More powerful.

And even though he was smiling, he hadn't
hugged her or kissed her cheek. In fact, he was
looking at her with a strange, watchful gaze. Her
own smile dimmed.

"What are you doing here, Brad?"

He smiled broadly. "Congratulate me, Sammy.
I met the girl of my dreams and she agreed to
marry me."

Dear Reader,

My, how time flies! I still remember the excitement of becoming Senior Editor for Silhouette Romance and the thrill of working with these wonderful authors and stories on a regular basis. My duties have recently changed, and I'm going to miss being privileged to read these stories before anyone else. But don't worry, I'll still be reading the published books! I don't think there's anything as reassuring, affirming and altogether delightful as curling up with a bunch of Silhouette Romance novels and dreaming the day away. So know that I'm joining you, even though Mavis Allen will have the pleasure of guiding the line now.

And for this last batch that I'm bringing to you, we've got some terrific stories! Raye Morgan is finishing up her CATCHING THE CROWN series with *Counterfeit Princess* (SR #1672), a fun tale that proves love can conquer all. And Teresa Southwick is just beginning her DESERT BRIDES trilogy about three sheiks who are challenged—and caught!—by American women. Don't miss the first story, *To Catch a Sheik* (SR #1674).

Longtime favorite authors are also back. Julianna Morris brings us *The Right Twin for Him* (SR #1676) and Doreen Roberts delivers *One Bride: Baby Included* (SR #1673). And we've got two authors new to the line—one of whom is new to writing! RITA® Award-winning author Angie Ray's newest book, *You're Marrying Her?*, is a fast-paced funny story about a woman who doesn't like her best friend's fiancée. And Patricia Mae White's first novel is about a guy who wants a little help in appealing to the right woman. Here *Practice Makes Mr. Perfect* (SR #1677).

All the best,

Mary-Theresa Hussey

Mary-Theresa Hussey
Senior Editor

Please address questions and book requests to:
Silhouette Reader Service
U.S.: 3010 Walden Ave., P.O. Box 1325, Buffalo, NY 14269
Canadian: P.O. Box 609, Fort Erie, Ont. L2A 5X3

You're Marrying *Her?*

ANGIE RAY

SILHOUETTE **Romance**®

Published by Silhouette Books

America's Publisher of Contemporary Romance

Barbara Benedict—thanks for walking
Sandra (Paul) Chvostal—thanks for talking
Colleen Adams—thanks for shopping
Mary-Theresa Hussey—thanks for chopping

SILHOUETTE BOOKS

ISBN 0-373-19675-X

YOU'RE MARRYING *HER?*

Copyright © 2003 by Angela Ray

ANGIE RAY

A RITA® Award-winning author for her first novel, Angie Ray has written historical and paranormal novels, but this is her first category romance. A native of Southern California, her mind is buzzing with ideas for stories, and she loves brainstorming while taking walks. Her husband and two children also provide plenty of distraction, but sooner or later she's always drawn back to her computer for "just one more scene"—which invariably leads to another book!

Dear Reader,

At age twelve, I regarded anything with the word *romance* in it with suspicion—until a friend gave me a category romance novel and I read it. I was hooked. Actually, I was addicted, obsessed and insatiable. I quickly figured out that the new series romances always appeared in the bookstore about the seventh of each month, but that sometimes they came earlier. Starting around the first, I would beg my poor mother to take me to the bookstore every day until those books showed up on the shelf.

My love affair with romances continued through high school, college, several jobs and even through my own personal romance with the man who would become my husband. I read romances before, during and after the birth of my two children (well, not actually on the delivery table, but you get the idea).

When I finally decided to write something myself, I wrote several historicals and time travels—but part of me was still drawn to the Silhouette Romance line and its simple (???!!!) stories about two people falling in love.

Writing this book was pure pleasure—as was working with the outstanding editorial staff at Silhouette (specifically, Mary-Theresa Hussey, my editor extraordinaire, and Shannon Godwin, her remarkable assistant).

Whether you're twelve or six times twelve, I hope you will have as much fun reading *You're Marrying* Her?, as I had writing it.

Sincerely,

Angie Ray

p.s. I love hearing from my readers! Please e-mail me at: ARay3@aol.com, or write to: P.O. Box 4672, Orange, CA 92863-4672.

Prologue

His lungs were on fire. Sweat dripped down his forehead, soaking the sweatband and trickling down into his eyes, clouding his vision. The cheers from the crowd on either side increased, the noise half obscured by the pounding of blood in his ears, but he knew why they were yelling. The finish line was only a few yards ahead.

Every part of him ached. He couldn't possibly go any faster—but he had to. Agonizing step after agonizing step, he drew closer to the figure ahead of him. He drew level. One more stride and he crossed the finish line—a nose ahead of the other man.

The crowd roared. Flags waved. Confetti floated through the air. "First place goes to...Brad Rivers!" boomed a voice over the loudspeaker.

The two men stopped jogging but kept walking to keep their muscles from cramping. They both breathed heavily. After a few minutes, the shorter one managed to gasp, "Damn...you...Brad, you beat me again!"

Brad laughed, even though his lungs burned with each exhalation. "I wasn't about to give up that trophy—I like the way it looks on my desk."

"You like taunting me with it, you mean." George Yorita, Brad's business partner and best friend, scowled, his thick black brows drawing together in a mock frown.

"C'mon, George. I never taunt."

"Then why do you start polishing the damn thing every time I come into your office?"

"Trophies need a lot of upkeep—"

George snorted. "Yeah, right." Before he could complain any more, a tiny Japanese-American woman with a toddler in tow came up. "I saw you running, Daddy," the three-year-old said. "How come you let Uncle Brad beat you?"

George smiled ruefully, hugging his wife and ruffling his son's hair at the same time. "Brad is very determined. When he wants something, he gets it."

"You're spoiled, Brad." Laura Yorita shook her head. "You can't always have everything you want."

"So far he has," George grumbled. "You should see the car he just bought. A '65 Mustang in mint condition. When he told me it was on eBay, I tried to bid on it but got locked out. A million people must have been trying for that car, but Brad somehow managed to get it. The prettiest little convertible I ever saw. Original seats, hubcaps, detailing—"

"Maybe you should stay here and salivate over Brad's car," Laura said sweetly, "while I take Collin home for his nap."

George grinned at his wife. "No, I'll come with

you. See you at the office Monday, Brad—but you better not drive that car. And you better not polish that trophy within my sight...."

Brad watched the three of them leave. Holding his son's hand, George bent to whisper in Laura's ear. She laughed and nodded. He put his arm around her waist and they continued on, George shortening his steps to match those of his wife and child.

A slight frown etched Brad's brow and he turned away, staring at the other runners crossing the finish line but not really seeing them. He hadn't always gotten what he wanted. There was one thing that continued to elude him....

"Water, mister?"

Brad took the proffered bottle, nodding his thanks to the race volunteer. Drinking the cold liquid, he turned his gaze back to the race.

Another runner had just crossed the finish line—a woman. She had a great figure, large breasts, small waist, curving hips, long legs. She looked familiar. He'd seen her somewhere before.

Yeah, now he remembered. At a party he'd attended a few weeks ago. The woman had been there. He hadn't paid too much attention to her then—beyond the obvious, that is.

"An actress," someone had told him.

He studied her more closely now. In addition to her other attributes, she had a beautiful face and carried herself with grace and self-assurance. She wore no engagement or wedding ring.

An idea sprang into his mind.

An insane idea. A completely ridiculous idea.

But then again, it had been an insane idea to start an electronics company just when all the tech stocks

were taking a dive. And it had been ridiculous to ex-
pand into e-business, just when all the dot-com's were
going belly-up.

In short, he would try. And he would succeed.

Because the truth of the matter was, in the end, he
always *did* get everything he wanted.

Chapter One

The wedding dress glowed in the late-afternoon sunlight streaming through the plate-glass windows of the small shop. Sequins formed a delicate tracery of vines on the bodice. A cluster of palest pink silk roses gathered the back of the full satin skirt into the faintest hint of a bustle. It was a Cinderella dress, symbolic of the bride's hopes for a happily-ever-after future with Prince Charming. Next week, a young woman would walk down the aisle in this dress and pledge the rest of her life to the man of her dreams.

Samantha Gillespie shuddered.

The reaction was involuntary. She really had nothing against marriage, Sam told herself as she studied the dress on the dais before her. It just wasn't something she wanted to do right now. Or any time soon. She was only twenty-four, for heaven's sake, and no matter what her mother said, Sam wasn't ready to get married yet. Not when life held such an endless array of possibilities. Why would she want to give that up for marriage?

"Well?" a voice demanded impatiently from the back of the shop. "Have you finished it?"

Sam glanced over her shoulder at the petite woman standing in the doorway of the small office at the far end of the showroom. "Almost," Sam told her sister. "I think it needs a few more clusters of roses at the back."

"For heaven's sake!" Dressed in a pastel-pink suit and frilly white blouse, Jeanette glared over the top of her chunky, black-rimmed reading glasses, her lips pursed. Samantha recognized the expression—and the suit. She'd tried to get Jeanette to wear something less insipid, more contemporary, but her sister refused to cooperate. "I can't wear that stuff you wear," Jeanette always said.

Which was completely unfair, Sam thought, tightening the knot of the shirt tied at her waist and smoothing her ancient blue jeans. The casual look might not suit Jeanette, but a deep red suit with a tailored cut would flatter her dark hair and eyes and make the most of her pleasingly plump figure.

"Why don't you let me make you a new suit?" Sam wheedled, ignoring Jeanette's disapproving expression. "We got in some red linen that would look gorgeous on you."

"No, thank you." Jeanette's toe, in a dull pink pump, tapped a stern tattoo. "I would prefer you worry about Miss Blogden's gown rather than my attire. She and her mother are supposed to be here in half an hour. Mrs. Blogden will be furious if the dress isn't finished."

"Don't worry." Samantha retrieved a sewing kit

and some pink silk from an antique armoire, then returned to the dais where the dress in question was reflected in a three-way mirror. "It won't take me long."

"Good grief, Sam!" Jeanette advanced from the office to the hat stand in the middle of the room—a more strategic spot for lecturing. "Must you always wait until the last minute? You know what Mrs. Blogden's like."

Sam sighed. Besides wearing boring clothes, Jeanette's favorite activity was to lecture Sam on her habit of procrastinating. Sam listened sometimes, and even made sporadic efforts to change, but somehow her bad habits always crept back.

"Don't worry," Sam said again. "The dress will be ready." Kneeling beside the mannequin, she twirled a piece of silk into a rose shape and stitched it onto the skirt of the wedding gown.

Jeanette chewed her lip. "I hate to leave you alone with her, but I promised Matt I'd come home early tonight."

"Oh?" Sam glanced sideways at her sister. "How *is* Matt?"

Jeanette's expression closed up. "He's fine," she said shortly.

Sam didn't press. She knew Jeanette and her husband had been arguing a lot lately, but Jeanette was as unrevealing as her suit when it came to talking about her marriage. Sam hoped the couple found some way to resolve their problems—for the sake of their three children if nothing else.

"Go on then," Sam told her. "Go home. Don't worry about Mrs. Blogden."

"I can't help worrying about Mrs. Blogden," Jea-

nette muttered. "I can't afford to lose any clients."
She straightened a veil on the hat stand. "By the way,
Brad Rivers called half an hour ago. He wanted to
talk to you."

"Brad?" Sam's thimble fell to the floor and rolled
off the dais, but she paid no attention. "What did he
want?"

"If you'd been here on time, you would know."

Sam rolled her eyes at her sister's back as Jeanette
retreated into her office. "Did he say anything?" she
called after her.

"Not really." Jeanette's muffled voice floated out.
"Just that he would call again later."

How odd. Sam crouched down to look for her thimble. She'd barely talked to Brad since Christmas,
eight months ago. She'd just returned to Southern
California after a two-year absence, and when she arrived—late—at her mother's house, she'd been delighted to see him. Only he hadn't been so happy to
see her. He'd been stiff, almost unfriendly. She'd
thought at first that her long absence was responsible
for his behavior. But as the day wore on and he didn't
loosen up, she'd realized something else was both-
ering him. She'd asked him flat out what was wrong,
but he'd said everything was fine.

She'd called him several times over the next several months and left messages, but some barrier remained. When he'd made some excuse not to come
to Easter dinner, everyone in her family had been surprised. He'd spent every holiday with them since Samantha was fourteen. And suddenly he couldn't come
because of "pressing demands at work"?

Hurt and confused, she'd stopped calling. He
hadn't made any effort to contact her. Until today.

Sam frowned at the rose she'd just sewn into place. What could he want to talk to her about now, after ignoring her for so long?

Jeanette came back out of her office with her purse and a stack of magazines. "Here are the latest bridal magazines. And something else I thought you'd like to see."

She held up a tabloid newspaper and Sam stared at the picture on the cover of a man splaying his hand outward in an effort to block his face from the camera.

Is This Man Too Good to Be True? screamed the headline.

In spite of his outstretched hand, Sam recognized him immediately. "Brad?" She reached for the tabloid. "Does this have something to do with why he called me?"

"Maybe." Jeanette held the magazine out of Sam's reach and flipped through the pages. "It says that he's selling RiversWare for $100 million and giving half the profits to his employees. Can you believe that?"

"He always was generous." Absently, Sam sewed another rose on the dress. "But what does that have to do with me?"

"It says in here somewhere...oh, here it is, listen to this—'although Rivers declined to be interviewed for this article, a reliable source tells us that he plans to use the money to convince his sweetheart to marry him!'" Jeanette lowered the newspaper and stared at Samantha. "He must mean you, Sammy."

Sam pricked her finger with the needle. Swearing under her breath, she sucked at the spot of blood before it could stain the white satin. "You're crazy.

Brad and I were never interested in each other. We were just friends.''

Jeanette snorted. "What guy is friends with a girl? Brad was in love with you."

"No, he wasn't. He was in love with Blanche Milken, remember?"

"Ha. He never cared about Blanche the way he did about you. He wasn't the same after you and Maria Vasquez left on that wild road trip cross-country— and you should have seen his face when Mom told him that you'd decided to go backpacking across Europe!"

"You should have seen his face when he saw me last Christmas!" Sam retorted. "The rocks at Stonehenge had more expression. He was not welcoming home his long-lost love, believe me."

"You always were blind about Brad. But I don't have time to argue with you. I've got to run." Jeanette set the magazines and tabloid on the floor. "It's past six o'clock. Come lock the door after I leave."

Sam automatically complied—Jeanette worried about Sam being alone in the shop after hours—then returned to where she'd been sitting, her brow furrowed. Blind about Brad? That wasn't true. Sam had known him better than anyone.

Her gaze drifted to the stack of magazines. The tabloid rested on top. Slowly, she picked up the newspaper and opened it. Inside was another picture, although the caption identified this one as being five years old. Brad stood with his hands shoved in the pants pockets of his ill-fitting brown polyester suit, his shoulders slightly hunched. His gray-blue eyes, the color obscured by the glasses he wore, gazed off into the distance as if contemplating some thorny dilemma.

Samantha smiled a little. She remembered that suit—he'd bought it at a thrift shop to wear to graduation. She recognized his pose, too—it was so typically Brad. The first time she'd seen him, when he moved in with his grandmother down the street from her parents' house, he'd been standing exactly the same way. He'd been seventeen, a senior in high school, quiet and serious. Only fourteen herself, she hadn't seen much of him until one day at school when she came upon some of the jocks—including her boyfriend, Pete—picking on him. Indignantly, she'd told them to knock it off.

Pete had been annoyed—he'd broken up with her a week later—but she hadn't really cared. She hadn't liked having a boyfriend, it was too restricting. But after that, she'd run into Brad a lot more often, and one day she impulsively invited him and his grandmother to Thanksgiving dinner. Her mother, whose rather abrasive personality was offset by her deep-seated maternal instincts, had taken him under her wing once she heard the story of how his parents and sister had been killed in a car crash. Brad—and his grandmother, before her death—had become part of the family.

Samantha put down the tabloid and sewed two more silk roses into place on the Blogden wedding dress. Even after Brad graduated and went to college, their friendship had continued and deepened. He'd helped her with some of her classes, and she'd made him laugh with her tales of trying to correct the fashion faux pas of her friends. He'd been one of the few people she could really talk to. She'd poured out her troubles and he'd always listened, ever sympathetic, ever patient. He wasn't like the boys in high school, the ones who got possessive after she dated them a few times. She'd always been able to count on Brad. She'd thought that they would be friends forever.

His behavior this last Christmas had come as a rude shock. Although she'd tried to pretend nothing was amiss, she'd been uneasy all evening. She'd drunk a little too much wine and chattered too much, acutely aware of his quietness, his stiffness, his *stillness*. She'd gotten the impression he wanted nothing to do with her, an impression reinforced by his reaction to her phone calls.

Frowning, Sam knotted and snipped the thread. So why did he want to talk to her now?

Brad was in love with you.

Jeanette's words echoed in Sam's brain. Automatically, she shook her head. Brad in love with her? The idea was laughable. They'd never even gone out on a date, let alone discussed marriage.

Well, okay, that wasn't strictly true. They *had* discussed it, the summer she'd graduated from high school. But only in the general sense. He'd asked her if she ever wanted to get married.

"Not until I'm really old," she'd said. "Thirty, at least." They'd ridden their bikes along Santa Monica Boulevard to the beach—her mother didn't like her to go alone—and she'd been sitting in the warm sand, under a strategically placed umbrella. Wearing a new polka-dot bikini, she'd been anxiously surveying her pale skin for signs of any new freckles.

Giving up on the inspection, she'd glanced up to find him staring at her. He'd looked away quickly, picking up a bottle of sunscreen.

"How about you?" She watched furtively as he rubbed the lotion onto his chest, the liquid mixing with the sprinkling of hair that had sprouted there in the last year or so. She wondered why he bothered. His skin browned easily, in spite of his light brown hair and gray-blue eyes.

"Yes. Someday." His elbows stuck up in the air as he applied lotion to his back. The muscles in his chest and arms—more defined than she remembered from the previous summer—rippled as he did so. "I want children. And a wife to come home to every night."

Sam wrinkled her nose. "Sounds boring. I want to travel. I want excitement. I want…" She looked up at the bright, cloudless blue sky, groping for words.

A seagull glided in the air, circling the beach, searching, waiting for an opportunity to swoop down and snatch some delicious morsel.

"You want what?" Brad asked.

The seagull dived. Descending with speed and grace, it focused completely on its target. Sam could imagine the wind rushing through its feathers, almost feel the bird's excitement as it swooped down, the rush of anticipation as it approached its goal.

The bird landed by a trash can. It pecked at the sandy remnants of a greasy, half-eaten hamburger. The prize secure in its beak, the seagull took off again.

Sam lay down on her towel and closed her eyes. "I don't know what I want yet," she told Brad. "But I will."

But now six years had passed, she was twenty-four, and she *still* didn't have a clue.

Shaking her head, Sam put her needle and thread

back in the sewing box and closed the lid. Maybe it was time she got a real job. She'd taken a couple of accounting classes before she quit college and had plenty of accounts receivable-payable experience both in the U.S. and in Europe. She should be able to find work fairly easily.

Or she could go back to college. She'd been considering that for the last year or so. She could finish her business degree while living off her share of the small trust fund her father had left. It would support her comfortably, if not luxuriously, while she studied.

Or she could continue to work for her sister. At least for a while. She'd taken the job with Jeanette partly to help out her sister, partly because she enjoyed working in the shop. But she knew Jeanette couldn't really afford to keep her on long-term. Sam needed to make some decision soon. Hopefully before Jeanette became completely fed up with her lack of punctuality and fired her.

A knock sounded at the door. Sam glanced at her watch. Seven o'clock—Mrs. Blogden had said she and her daughter would be at the shop by six-thirty. Jeanette should have stayed and lectured *them,* Sam thought. Although, of course, Jeanette would never criticize a client. Only sisters enjoyed that privilege.

The knock came again.

Reluctantly she stood up, fluffing up her curls and brushing the stray bits of thread and cloth from her shirt and jeans. She picked up the stack of magazines and put them in the armoire before walking toward the door.

Another knock sounded, more impatient this time.

"Hold on to your horses," Samantha muttered, but

she arranged her features in a smile as she opened the door. "Your dress is ready...."

The man standing on the threshold arched an eyebrow, his gray-blue eyes smiling down at her.

"You always did have a peculiar idea of me, Sammy."

Chapter Two

Samantha stared up at the man in shock. *Brad?*
She'd seen him just eight months ago, but he
looked...different. Incredibly different. His glasses
were gone, he wore a dark gray pin-striped suit that
looked tailormade and silver cuff links. His sun-
streaked hair was expertly cut, his nails manicured.
On his wrist, he wore a gold Rolex watch, and on his
feet, polished to a brilliant shine, shoes that screamed
custom-made Italian leather.

But the difference went beyond clothes. He smelled
of expensive gabardine, fine linen and spicy cologne.
He was still tall and lean, but his shoulders looked
broader. More powerful.

"A peculiar idea?" she replied stupidly, distracted
by her efforts to decide whether his shoulders actually
were wider or if the expensive jacket just made them
appear so.

"I may have done some wild things in my life, but
I draw the line at wearing ladies' dresses."

Her gaze flew to his. His gray-blue eyes held a glint. A *familiar* glint.

She started to smile. "What wild thing have you ever done, Brad? Ditched class to work on some computer program?"

"Oh, you'd be surprised," he said, the glint still in his eyes.

She laughed. Her first impression that he'd changed faded away. *This* was the Brad she remembered from high school. Someone she could laugh with. Her friend.

Or so she'd thought. He certainly hadn't acted very friendly in the past eight months. And even though he was smiling, he hadn't hugged her or kissed her cheek. In fact, he was looking at her with a strange, watchful gaze. Her own smile dimmed. "What are you doing here, Brad?"

His gaze didn't waver. "I need to talk to you. I was going to call again, but I realized that this is too important to tell you over the phone, so I decided it would be better to come and see you in person."

Too important to tell her over the phone? Sam stared at him uneasily, Jeanette's words popping into her brain.

Brad was in love with you.

Sam tried to banish the foolish thought. He'd barely spoken to her in the past eight months. That was hardly a sign of love.

But the thought refused to go away. Could Jeanette have been right, after all? Had Brad come to propose? "You're wearing a suit," she said, trying to hide her uneasiness. "Very nice. Are you trying to impress someone?"

"You, I hope."

Her hand tightened on the doorknob. "I'm duly impressed," she said, as lightly as possible.

"Are you?" The watchful expression in his eyes turned into something even more obscure and unreadable. "May I come in?"

"Oh, of course." The pitch of her laughter a bit high, she stepped back and allowed him to enter the shop.

He looked around with interest, his gaze taking in the forest-green sofa and the pine table littered with catalogs and pattern books, the peach-colored wallpaper with its tiny white flowers and the rainbow of dresses hanging on one wall. His eyes lingered on the mannequin with Miss Blogden's dress.

"Did you make this, Sammy?"

She nodded, unable to prevent a small welling of pride at the admiration in his voice. She'd done most of the sewing herself, endured thousands of pinpricks. But the result was worth it.

"You always did have a talent with clothes," he said. "Remember that outfit you gave me one Christmas? A pair of baggy shorts, a black T-shirt and silver-rimmed sunglasses—along with a little note suggesting that I grow a goatee."

She couldn't help smiling. "Okay, so maybe I wasn't very subtle. I still think you would've looked great. You could have at least tried the outfit. You never wore it even once."

"Not my style." He glanced at the row of gowns against the wall. "Do you make all the dresses for the shop?"

"Good heavens, no. Most of them are off the rack," she said. "I only make a dress once in a while when a customer requests something unique. Usually,

I just help Jeanette with whatever needs to be done. She's doing very well. She only started a year ago, but she's already close to making a profit. She had six weddings in June, and has at least two scheduled every month for the next year. I just assisted her with a wedding at the Arboretum in Arcadia with ten bridesmaids and ten groomsmen, a harpist, programs, the works. It was beautiful, we released 10,000 Monarch butterflies after the ceremony—"

She stopped, suddenly aware that she was babbling. "I'm sorry. I didn't mean to ramble on."

"I enjoy listening to you. I remember Jeanette talking about starting a bridal shop ten years ago."

"I didn't think she'd ever actually own one. She hit a few roadblocks."

"That's normal. The important thing is she didn't give up."

"Mmm." She glanced at him. "Is that what you wanted to talk to me about? Jeanette's shop?"

His mouth quirked. "You always were direct, Sam. To tell you the truth, I came here for another reason. There's something I want to ask you...."

She stiffened, unable to prevent herself. "Oh?"

His gaze traveled over her face. "Yes," he said gently. "I want to apologize for my behavior over the last several months. I was...disturbed about a certain situation and I allowed that to affect my friendships."

"Oh, Brad!" The tension flowed out of her. She touched his arm lightly. "Have you been able to fix the situation?"

"No, but I'm working on it." He smiled down at her. "In the meantime, I wanted to ask if we could be friends again."

"That would be wonderful." She smiled back at

him, absently noticing that the angle of his chin seemed more pronounced than she remembered, the texture of skin at his jaw a little rougher. A few lines in his forehead were now permanent. "I've missed you."

"Have you?" He reached out and brushed a curl off her forehead, his fingers lingering on her skin. "I thought you'd forgotten about me completely."

"I could never do that." His touch was friendly, the warmth from his fingers penetrating her skin and deep inside her. "You're the nicest guy I've ever known. I've always thought of you as my best friend."

Abruptly, his hand dropped to his side. For an instant, she saw something in his eyes, a spark of emotion she couldn't identify. He grinned. "I'm glad to hear it—it will make my next question a lot easier."

Her tension returned. Had she relaxed too soon?

He laughed, but his eyes still had that spark. "Don't look like that, Sammy. It's nothing terrible. At least, I hope you won't think it's terrible."

Oh, dear heaven. "Brad, I don't think—"

"Please, Sammy. Just listen. I've wanted to get married for a long time—"

Her fingernails bit into the palms of her hands. She couldn't believe it. He really was going to propose. Her stomach churned. "Oh, Brad...."

"And I've finally found someone who will have me."

"I'm afraid—" She stopped, blinking in confusion. "What did you say?"

He smiled broadly. "Congratulate me, Sammy. I met the girl of my dreams and she has agreed to marry me. Her name is Heather Lovelace. And she's the sweetest, kindest, most beautiful woman in the world."

Samantha couldn't speak. She felt dizzy for a second. Brad was getting married? She had never thought...that is, she couldn't quite imagine...

"And we want you to design the dress. And Jeanette to arrange the wedding. Will you do it? Sammy? Sammy? Are you all right?"

"I'm fine." She shook her head, trying to clear away the unaccountable vertigo that had made everything in the shop tilt sideways. She forced herself to smile and say, "Of course I'll do it. And I'm sure Jeanette can handle the wedding. If she can't, I'll do it myself," she promised recklessly.

His eyes crinkled at the corners. "Thank you, Sammy. Heather's waiting out in the car right now. She wants to meet you. Will you come to dinner with us?"

"Oh, no, I couldn't." Her refusal was automatic and instinctive. She didn't feel very well. Maybe she had a summer cold coming on.

"Why not?"

"I...I couldn't go to dinner dressed like this."

"Come on, Sammy. You look great."

"You're wearing a suit—"

"There has to be a dress you could wear somewhere in this place."

There was, of course. She bit her lip. What was wrong with her? She'd just been thinking how much she wanted to be friends with Brad again, and now here he was, wanting to renew their old relationship and share his happy news.

And it was happy news. She couldn't quite figure out why it was affecting her so strangely. She was happy for Brad. Wasn't she? Of course she was. He was going to get married and live happily ever after.

If that was possible.

She'd seen married people in action. She'd seen how couples could fight and tear each other apart. That was why Brad's news unsettled her—she was worried about him. She didn't want him to have to experience that unpleasantness.

"I really can't. I'm expecting a client." She glanced at her watch. It was almost seven-thirty. Apparently Mrs. Blogden wasn't going to show.

"Can't you call and cancel? Please, Sammy."

"Well…" She wavered. She did want to meet Brad's fiancée. Heather Lovelace. The most beautiful woman in the world, Brad had called her. But Sam took that with a grain of salt. Brad was in love with Heather after all. He'd also described her as sweet and kind. That sounded like Blanche Milken, the girl he'd had a crush on in high school. Blanche had been a straight-A student with mousy, colorless clothes to go along with her mousy, colorless personality.

"Okay," Samantha said, making up her mind. "Let me change and call Mrs. Blogden to make sure she isn't coming. It'll only take me a few minutes."

"Great. I'll go tell Heather. Come outside when you're ready."

He left, and Sam went into the office to call Mrs. Blogden. The housekeeper answered and informed Sam that Mrs. Blogden was at a party and wouldn't be home until late. Sam wasn't too surprised. Mrs. Blogden frequently didn't show up for her appointments and rarely called to cancel.

Her conscience clear, Sam grabbed a short black dress off a rack, went into the dressing room and changed. Quickly, she slipped on some strappy, high-heeled sandals that increased her height from an insignificant five three to a much more respectable five six.

She brushed out her hair, applied enough makeup to conceal her freckles and surveyed herself in the mirror. Acceptable, she thought. The black matte jersey echoed the sheen of her dark curls and made her eyes seem more green than gold. She hurried outside.

A red sports car was parked there. Next to it stood Brad, his arm around the waist of a tall, slender blonde dressed in a form-fitting halter dress of glittering bronze.

Samantha stumbled on the asphalt. *This* was his fiancée? The woman was gorgeous! Not a day over eighteen, she had the long, lean look of a model—except for the large, firm breasts that threatened to bounce right out of her low-cut dress. She was wearing heels, too, fantastic purple-and-bronze Jimmy Choo stilettos that lifted her at least four inches over Sam's suddenly pathetic height. Sam felt like a troll next to her.

This was no Blanche Milken.

Sam pinned a smile to her lips and held out her hand. "Hi, Heather, I'm Samantha Gillespie."

The blonde ignored her outstretched hand. A cloud of Chanel No. 5 enveloped Sam as Heather hugged her. "Samantha! Brad has told me so much about you!"

"He has?" Sam murmured faintly when she could speak.

Heather smiled blindingly. Her teeth were as white and perfect as the rest of her. "Oh, yes. I have to admit that when he first told me what good friends you were, I was the tiniest bit jealous, but now that I've met you, I can see that I didn't need to worry at all.''

Startled, Sam glanced at Heather's face. Had the woman—girl, really—meant that the way it sounded?

Heather was smiling, her large blue eyes clear and innocent.

Brad smiled, too. ''I told you you were being silly. Samantha and I have always been just friends. Right, Sam?''

''Right.'' *You're being oversensitive,* Sam told herself sternly. She smiled at Brad's fiancée. ''You're marrying a really nice guy.''

''Nice?'' Heather turned to Brad and drew a teasing finger down his chest. ''I don't know if I would have used exactly that word to describe you, darling.''

Sam frowned at the sexual implication of the blonde's words. She glanced at Brad, expecting him to defend his character, but he only gazed at Heather, his hand closing over the blonde's. The two of them stared into each other's eyes, a silent communication of some shared memory passing between them. They appeared to have completely forgotten Sam's presence.

She cleared her throat.

The spell was broken. The two lovers stepped away from each other. Brad glanced at Sam, his mouth curving ruefully. ''Sorry. You know what it's like to be in love.''

Sam forced herself to smile again, but inwardly she felt oddly defensive. Of course she knew what it was like. She'd had innumerable boyfriends in high school and college. She'd gone out with men from here to Chicago to New York to London, Paris and Rome.

But somehow, none of them had ever looked at her the way Brad looked at Heather. Sam didn't remember him ever looking at Blanche Milken that way. Talk about wearing your heart on your sleeve. She would've thought he would show more restraint.

"Shall we go?" she asked brightly.

Brad opened the passenger door.

"You don't mind if I sit in the front, do you?" Heather asked Sam. "My legs get terribly cramped in the back."

Sam saw Brad's gaze go immediately to the impossibly long legs of his fiancée. "Of course not," she said, feeling like a child relegated to the back seat. She climbed into the tight space behind Heather and Brad.

With a roar of the powerful engine, they were off.

Chapter Three

Samantha sat at the dinner table of the West L.A. restaurant, watching the laughing couple across from her. They seemed giddy with happiness. There was a glow in Brad's eyes that she'd never seen before—except, perhaps, when he was working on some complicated project. But this wasn't the same. A sense of electricity seemed to envelop him.

Heather glowed, too. Sam had never met a woman who glowed so much.

Sam looked down at her menu and tried to subdue the wave of dislike she felt for Heather. So far, she'd seen nothing about the blonde that would justify Brad's falling in love with her. Except for her gorgeous face and figure. But Heather must have more to her than that. Brad wasn't the kind of man to care only about a woman's looks.

Sam shifted her gaze to Brad as he raised a finger and a waiter rushed over. Watching him place their order, she was struck once again by a sense that he had changed—and not just on the surface.

Sam could restrain her curiosity no longer. "What happened to you, Brad?" she asked after the waiter left. "You used to be a strictly meat and potatoes man and now you're ordering shrimp and jicama. And you look like you should be on the cover of *GQ*. Isn't that an Armani suit?"

"Heather happened to me." Putting his arm around his fiancée, he smiled down at her. "She convinced me to try some new dishes and helped me make a few changes—new clothes, haircut and contact lenses. An improvement, don't you think, Sammy?"

"I always thought you looked fine." Forgetting her own attempts to change Brad's wardrobe, Sam realized suddenly that she really didn't care for this new style that Heather had foisted on him. Before, he'd looked like…Brad. Now he looked almost alien. He looked rich. Sophisticated. Masculine.

She shook her head. Brad was Brad, no matter how he dressed. That much she was sure of.

Heather had arched her brows at Sam's response. "I think appearance is extremely important. Some women, especially older ones, don't set any standards for themselves at all. I'm always careful to wear the right clothes and makeup and watch my weight. I count every calorie. I think it's worth it, don't you, Brad?"

Brad's gaze wandered over Heather's magnificent figure. "Sure, sweetheart."

Heather beamed.

A waiter passed by with a dessert tray, and Sam resisted an urge to seize a slice of strawberry torte and stuff it down Heather's throat. Instead she told herself that Heather probably hadn't meant to imply that Sam was old and fat. Forcing herself to smile politely, she asked, "So, how did you two meet?"

"At the RiversWare Run," Brad said. "Heather loves to run and enters competitions whenever she can."

Heather sipped her drink. "Do you run, Samantha?"

"Not if I can avoid it." Sam tried to remember exactly when the RiversWare Run had been. About four months ago, she was pretty sure. That wasn't very long.

"Running doesn't appeal to everyone," Heather said in a kindly manner. "I like to try something different once in a while, too. Like in-line skating. I started just a few weeks ago. Brad says I'm a real fast learner."

"Heather's amazing on skates," Brad interjected. "I've never seen anyone as graceful as she is."

Heather smiled modestly. "In-line skating's very easy. Even the biggest klutz imaginable can do it."

"Sam can't," Brad announced cheerfully.

Sam's fingernails curled into her napkin.

Heather's eyes widened. "You can't?"

Sam could barely stay upright on skates and usually wouldn't have minded admitting it. But something about the blonde's incredulous blue eyes made Sam say, "Of course I can." She looked past Heather to the approaching waiter. "Oh, here comes our food."

Brad wasn't diverted, however. Releasing Heather's hand so the waiter could put their plates down, he stared at Sam. "Since when? That time I took you skating, you almost fell on your face."

"That was a long time ago. I've improved," Sam

lied. She remembered the time he referred to very well. It had been a high school fund-raiser, and she'd been falling all over the place until Brad came to her rescue. He'd helped her up and held her upright—until someone brushed by them, knocking her off balance. Legs and arms sprawling, they'd both ended up on the floor. Tangled together, they'd started laughing uncontrollably. By the end of the evening, they'd both had more bruises than two boxers—not to mention a bad case of the hiccups.

"Unfortunately, I can't go skating very often," Sam added as she cut a bite of chicken and swished it in mango-chili sauce. "Helping at Jeanette's shop takes up all my time."

"I work, too," Heather said. "But I still find time to exercise."

"Keeping fit is very important in Heather's business," Brad explained. "She's an actress."

Heather preened. "I just had a part in a special TV movie called *Baywatch—the California Reunion.*"

"Oh, really?" Sam had never watched the show, but she knew it was something about lifeguards at the beach. "That must have been exciting."

"Yes, it was. David Hasselhoff himself rescued me when a great white shark attacked the swimmers in the middle of an earthquake right after a deranged yoga instructor blew up the pier. I didn't have any speaking lines, but I did have to scream very loudly. Jim, the director, is editing the final cut of the movie right now, so I'm on call. That's why I'm staying at the hotel across the street, because it's close to the location shoot."

"You're not staying with Brad?"

"My house is too inconvenient," Brad said.

Sam, chewing on a bite of risotto with pine nuts and green chilies, was surprised but strangely relieved. The thought of him living with Heather was very distasteful. The thought of him sleeping with her…

The rice and pine nuts in her stomach oscillated.

Forcing herself to keep her tone pleasant, Sam asked Heather, "When will the movie be on TV?"

"Not for several months," Heather said. "But my agent says the offers will pour in once it airs. Not that I'll accept any of them, of course."

"Why not?" Sam asked.

"Because I'm marrying Brad. I want nothing more than to be his wife, to love him and support him with every fiber of my being. And, if God is willing, I will bear his children, the precious fruit of our deep and eternal love for each other."

Sam smiled, thinking the blonde was joking. But her smile faded when she saw Brad wasn't laughing. He was gazing tenderly at his fiancée, who gazed back worshipfully.

Sam gagged on her mango-chili sauce.

Her cough broke the spell. "Are you all right?" Heather asked.

"Mmm." She coughed once more to clear her throat and to prevent any resumption of adoring gazing. "Brad said you wanted me to design your dress."

"Oh, yes," Heather said. "It would mean so much to Brad and me. Do you think you can do it?"

"Of course," Sam said automatically. "You must come to my sister's shop tomorrow and we can look through the catalogs."

Heather tapped a French-manicured nail against her chin. "Well…I hope you don't mind…but I would really like something unique. Something that suits my personality."

Something with lots of frills and lace. *And maybe a big lollipop.* The bitchy thought popped into Sam's head before she could prevent it.

"Oh, that reminds me," Heather said, laying down her fork. "I promised to call my agent about a possible part playing a housewife in a commercial. He thinks I would be perfect for it." Her eyelashes fluttered in response to Brad's warm look. "I'll be back in a minute, darling."

She rose and glided gracefully away.

Sam watched her go, wondering how on earth the girl got her hips to sway like that.

She peeked at Brad to see his reaction. To her surprise, he was looking straight at her, paying no attention to Heather's hips. A crooked smile quirked the corner of his mouth.

"So, what do you think?" His gaze was strangely intent as he asked the question.

"She's..." Sam paused, several unkind remarks hovering on her tongue. She took a deep breath. "She's perfect," she admitted. "I'm sure you'll be very happy, Brad."

Brad leaned back against his seat, his face expressionless for a long moment. Then he smiled. "She's amazing, isn't she? I couldn't believe my luck when she said yes to my proposal." He stirred some cream into his coffee. "What about you, Sam? Are you seeing anyone?"

"No, not right now. I've been too busy at the shop."

"Oh, yes, the shop. Are you planning on working there permanently?"

"No," she said. "Not really. I'll probably look for some other job soon."

"Still haven't made up your mind what you want to do with your life?"

Samantha pushed her rice around on her plate. "Not yet. I never could figure out what I wanted. Unlike you. You always knew, didn't you, Brad?"

"Yes, I did. I still do."

She'd never paid much attention before, but he really had the most determined chin she'd ever seen—a square jaw ending in a resolute knob. There was no softness beneath, no cleft to compromise it. "You've done very well for yourself. You've accomplished a lot."

He shrugged. "A case of being in the right place at the right time."

"You're too modest."

"So Heather tells me." He grinned. "She's an extraordinary woman. I really am the luckiest man alive."

"I think Heather's the lucky one."

He leaned forward in his seat, his gaze intent. "Do you, Sam?"

"Of course. You're my friend."

He leaned back. He wiped his mouth with his napkin, then held out his hand. "Best friends, right?"

Nodding, she put her hand in his. They sat there for a moment, smiling at each other. His hand was much larger than hers, warm and strong.

Suddenly, for no reason she could think of, Sam felt like crying.

"Sam?" His fingers tightened on hers. "Are you okay?"

Sam blinked hard. "I'm fine." But she had to force herself to smile.

Brad's gaze went to her mouth, then flickered back up. "Uh, Sam…I hope you don't mind me mentioning it, but you've got a green chili stuck in your teeth."

Sam stopped smiling immediately. Licking her teeth with her tongue, she wondered uneasily how long the chili had been there.

Please don't let Heather have seen it, she prayed silently. "Is it gone?" she asked, parting her lips again.

He shook his head. "Looks like it's wedged in there pretty good."

She stood up and put her napkin on her chair. "Please excuse me," she muttered.

Weaving in between the tables toward the rear of the restaurant, she continued to try to find the chili with her tongue.

She entered the rest room, bared her teeth into the mirror, but saw no sign of any chilies. She must have gotten it out on the way, she thought.

She washed her hands, glad for the small respite to try to make sense of her fluctuating emotions. Ever since she'd heard of Brad's plans to marry, she'd felt a bit off balance, a little shaky inside. Perhaps because in some odd way, she'd always thought of Brad as *hers.* Her rock. Her anchor. Her friend. She'd thought that nothing would ever change that. But she knew, without a doubt, that once he married Heather, everything would change. Everything would be completely different.

She washed her hands again, trying to banish the tears prickling at the back of her eyes. Really, she was being incredibly foolish and selfish. She and Brad could still be friends. She was happy for him. She *was*.

Feeling more in control, she held her palms under the dryer, muttering to herself, "I *am* happy for them. I *am* happy for them."

Her nose twitched a little as she smelled cigarette smoke. It seemed as if someone was always lighting up in the bathroom, trying to circumvent the no-smoking laws. "I *am* happy for them...."

A toilet flushed, and the door to one of the stalls opened to reveal Heather.

"Oh, it's you," the younger woman said. "I thought I was about to be busted." Opening her tiny evening bag, she pulled out another cigarette and lit it. "You want one?"

"No, thank you," Sam said automatically, hiding her surprise. With a cigarette in her hand, Heather didn't appear nearly as young and sweet as she had in the restaurant. "Brad must have changed more than I thought—he used to hate smoking."

"Are you kidding?" Heather snorted, smoke blowing from her nostrils. "He's such a health freak, he'd probably break our engagement if he found out."

"He doesn't know?"

"Of course not. I'm not a fool. You won't tell him, will you?"

Sam stared at her. Surely the girl couldn't be serious? "I would think he could smell the smoke on your breath."

"Oh, I'm very careful, don't worry."

"I'm not worried—that is, I'm sure Brad loves you enough that he won't care that you smoke." Sam gave Heather a strained smile and tried to make a joke. "Although he may insist that you quit when you start having children."

"Children—ha! I detest the creatures. No way am I going to have a passel of brats. They'd ruin my figure—not to mention my career."

"But...but I thought you were giving up your career."

"I had to tell Brad that, or he never would've proposed. He wants a little woman who will adore him. But I have plans of my own and no man is going to stand in my way."

"Why are you marrying him, then?"

Heather looked at her as though she were a mental case. "Are you crazy? He's incredibly attractive, straight and rich. With $100 million, he can help finance a movie for me so I won't have to do these crummy little commercials anymore."

Sam couldn't stop staring at her. The only thing she could think to say was "He'll only have $50 million once he gives half to his employees."

Ashes fell from Heather's cigarette to the pristine marble floor. "God, are you naive. You don't really think I would allow him to do that? You really fell for my little act in there, didn't you? I thought another woman would see through that pack of lies immediately. So, what are you going to do now? Tattle to Brad?"

"Brad's my friend."

Heather laughed—an ugly, distorted sound. "Don't tell me—you're one for all and all for one, or some crap like that, right? God, what century were you born in? Tell him whatever you like—he'll never believe you." She cast a sly sideways look at Sam. "He's so besotted, he would never take someone else's word over mine."

"You think so?"

"I know so, sweetie." Heather stubbed out the cigarette on the floor. "Don't try to make trouble for me—or you'll regret it."

Heather popped several breath mints in her mouth, then glided out of the bathroom. Sam stood where she was, staring at the crushed cigarette butt on the floor. She felt like she'd wandered into a soap opera—with Heather playing the part usually reserved for Susan Lucci.

In something of a daze, Sam walked back to the table. She spent the next half hour watching Heather smile and laugh and press up against Brad as if she thought he was the most wonderful man in the world. No one watching her would ever doubt that she was deeply, wholeheartedly in love with the man at her side.

Sam could barely doubt it herself. The scene in the bathroom was beginning to take on a surreal quality— it seemed like a bad dream. Could she have imagined it?

Heather glanced over at her. For an instant, a cat-like smile curved her lips. Then it vanished and she was gazing up at Brad, the adoration back in her eyes.

Sam's lips tightened. No, she hadn't imagined it. Without a doubt, the blonde was the greediest, most conniving female she'd ever met. Sam wouldn't have believed such an amoral person existed if she hadn't heard the evidence with her own ears. Heather didn't care about Brad at all—she cared only about his money.

Sam's gaze flickered to Brad. He smiled down into

Heather's eyes, completely unaware of her deceit. Poor Brad. Did he have any idea what he was getting himself into? No, of course not. Poor, poor, poor Brad.

He thought Heather was perfect. He was in love with her. He would be devastated when he found out the truth. Sam hated to think of him being hurt like that.

Memories flashed through her brain—memories of Brad listening while she ranted and raved about Joe Danvers's jerkiness. Joe had dumped her because she wouldn't have sex with him, and her pride had been hurt more than her heart, but still Brad had listened and supported her decision.

Brad had always been there for her. If it hadn't been for him, she never would have gotten through calculus in college. She'd had little aptitude for math, but he'd explained the theorems over and over until she'd understood.

He'd been there, too, when her parents divorced, and then, a year later, when her father died. She'd cried on his shoulder, and he'd rocked her and smoothed her hair back from her face and held her tightly. The warmth of his arms around her had helped banish the coldness, given her strength to go on.

Brad was a nice guy. The nicest guy she'd ever known. He didn't deserve a piece of work like Heather.

Brad bent over to whisper something in the blonde's ear. As if reading Sam's thoughts, Heather stared at her, her gaze mocking.

Sam clenched her teeth until they ached. She couldn't let Brad ruin his life. He was her friend. She had to do something to save him. He *needed* her.

She wasn't going to let him down.

Chapter Four

The easiest course of action would be to have a talk with Brad and tell him what Heather had said to her, Sam decided. The blonde was unbelievably arrogant—did she really think that Brad would believe her over his old friend, Sam?

Therefore, when the meal was finished and Brad suggested dropping Heather off at her hotel before driving Sam home, she was delighted.

Heather's eyes narrowed, but all she said was "Hurry back, Brad. I have a present for you—a surprise."

The way the woman was licking her lips made Sam think that the "surprise" wouldn't be a new one. Brad probably wouldn't care about anything once the blonde got her hands on him.

The thought was an unpleasant one. *Extremely* unpleasant. It was still gnawing at Sam a few minutes later when she was in the car with Brad speeding down the freeway. She supposed it was foolish to be bothered by the thought of Brad and Heather having sex. They were two normal, healthy adults who planned to get married. Heather didn't exactly look like Little Bo Peep, and she'd made it clear that she found Brad attractive. *Incredibly* attractive, she'd called him. How strange. Sam never thought of him that way.

"Isn't Heather fantastic?" Brad's voice broke the silence. "I still can't believe she agreed to marry me."

"I can." Sam couldn't prevent the slightly sarcastic note from creeping into her voice.

Brad gave her a quick sideways glance before returning his gaze to the lane of traffic before him. "What do you mean, Sammy? You said yourself she's perfect."

"No one is perfect. I think *interesting* might be a better word for Heather."

"Interesting?" Brad's eyebrows rose. "That sounds like someone describing a blind date. Come on, tell me what you really think."

Watching his expression in the dim glare from the passing streetlights, Sam said carefully, "She seemed a little different when we were in the bathroom."

"Different in what way?"

"Not quite as friendly."

Brad exited the freeway and braked at a stoplight. He turned to face Sam. "There's something you have to understand about Heather. She's really gotten a raw deal from other women. Most of them dislike her because of her looks and try to undermine her. You wouldn't believe some of the stories they've made up about her. One woman actually tried to make me believe that Heather was only interested in my money!

I had considered the woman a friend, but after that, I broke off contact with her.''

Sam gaped at him.

''I can see you're as shocked as I was,'' Brad said. ''And I'm sure you'll agree that it's no wonder Heather sometimes seems a little wary. I told her you weren't like that, though. I told her you would never say bitchy, malicious things about her behind her back.''

''No. No, of course I wouldn't,'' Sam managed to say. She couldn't believe it—Heather had made it virtually impossible for Sam to say anything bad about her! The blonde was extraordinarily devious.

The light changed and the car moved forward again. Sam gazed out the window at the passing cars, silently cursing Heather's cleverness. She would have to proceed cautiously. ''But have you ever wondered if some of the things those women said might be true?''

''Absolutely not. Oh, I realize she might seem a bit standoffish when you first meet her, but that's because she's actually very shy.''

Shy? Oh, *please.* Why were men such fools over a pretty face and a gorgeous body? ''You've known her how long—four months?'' In spite of her inner thoughts, Sam managed to keep her voice neutral.

''We've been dating almost two months.''

''Two months! That's not very long at all!''

''It may not seem long, but I feel as though I've known her all my life.''

Sam stared at him. Lights speeding past the car backlit his strong profile, but she could not make out his expression. Could he really believe such baloney?

Heather really had her claws into him. Exactly how deeply was beginning to worry Sam more and more.

"I saw an article about you in the paper," she said, deciding to try a more subtle approach.

He grimaced. "The one that made me sound like a cross between a lunatic and a saint? I simply decided sharing the profits was the right thing to do. Everyone has worked hard—they deserve part of the rewards." He glanced at her sideways. "Do *you* think I'm a fool?"

"Not at all. I think it's extremely generous of you." She fiddled with her seat belt. "What does Heather think?"

"Heather is happy whatever I do. She only asked that I wait to give the money away until after we're married so she can be part of it."

Sam's antennae went up. If the two of them were married, would the money become community property? "Do you have a prenuptial agreement?" she blurted out.

Brad looked at her reproachfully. "Of course not. Oh, she offered to. But I trust Heather. I would never ask her to sign something that implied otherwise."

Sam bit her lip. Heather had second-guessed Brad perfectly, and he'd fallen for it. The blonde was right—he wasn't going to believe anything Sam told him.

Something squeezed at her heart. Once, he would have believed anything she'd told him—he'd trusted her completely. But now it seemed he placed a higher value on Heather's word than Sam's.

Of course, a man *should* believe his future wife above all others. But Sam couldn't help but feel a pang of longing for the old days, when her position as Brad's friend had been uncontested. She felt…usurped.

He parked in an impossibly tight space and walked her to her front door. She fumbled with her keys, then turned to face him. "Brad…"

He was standing closer than she expected. "Yes?"

She inched back slightly, her shoulder blades brushing against the door, so that she could look up at him without craning her neck. "Heather is…" She paused, searching for the right words.

"Yes?" he said.

"Heather is the kind of woman that men find very attractive."

"Yeah, I'll agree with that."

"I hope…well, I just hope you haven't confused sex with love."

"Ah." He gave her an unreadable look. "Is there that much difference between the two?"

"Of course there is!" she said indignantly. "Sex is temporary. Love is forever."

"I see. And you're basing your opinion on your vast experience?"

"Yes…no…I mean, this has nothing to do with me—"

"But it does. I need to know how valid your advice is. Are you trying to tell me that clown you brought home last Christmas was a great lover, but not great husband material?"

"Of course not! Jean-Paul and I never…" She stopped biting her lip.

"You never what? Never had sex? I knew that."

"What do you mean, you knew that?" The calm certainty in his voice irritated her. "You know nothing about my relationship with Jean-Paul."

"I know *you.* And I know you're afraid of sex."

"Afraid of sex! What are you talking about? I'm not afraid of sex!"

"No? I'd be willing to bet RiversWare, my house, hell, even my car that you're still a virgin."

Her face burned. "That's none of your business," she informed him. "I don't know how we got so far off the subject—"

"You were lecturing me about not confusing love and sex with regards to Heather." He was smiling— an annoying, obnoxious, self-satisfied smile. "Don't worry. Heather and I haven't made love yet. She wants to wait for the wedding night."

"She does?" Sam almost dropped her keys. "And you agreed?"

He nodded. "I'm willing to wait for the woman I want."

His words were quiet, but they caused a peculiar pang in Sam's heart. Brad was...he was so darn *good.*

She looked up at him, considering what to say. His eyes were in shadow, his expression obscured—not that she would have been able to tell what he was thinking, anyway. He'd always been hard to read. Light glanced along his jaw, drawing her gaze. A man with a chin like his wouldn't easily be persuaded that he'd made a mistake. But she had to try.

"I don't want to say anything bad about Heather...but I'm afraid she just isn't good enough for you."

He moved a little closer, his shoulders blocking the streetlight and casting his face into shadow. "Oh? Who do you think is good enough for me?"

"I don't know." She was aware of the smell of

gabardine again. The scent made it difficult for her to think. "Someone like…like…Blanche Milken."

"You think I belong with someone like Blanche Milken instead of Heather?" Even in the dim light, Sam saw his eyes narrow. "Are you trying to imply that I'm not man enough for Heather?"

"No, of course not—"

"Sam, go inside. Now."

Something in his voice made her scuttle inside. Lifting the curtain, she peered through the window. She watched his tall, dark figure stride to the car and get inside. She heard the door slam, the roar of an engine, then the screech of tires as he took off down the street.

She dropped the curtain, her brow furrowed. What was *wrong* with him? He'd seemed angry. Only, Brad never got angry. But he'd been strange all evening—dressed in a suit, making goo-goo eyes at Heather, accusing Sam of being afraid of sex….

Afraid of sex! What a ridiculous thing to say. And although it was true she hadn't slept with any of the boys—men—she'd gone out with, it wasn't because she was afraid. She simply wasn't ready to tie herself down yet. She knew sex was the first step toward acquiring a ring, a mortgage and a bagful of diapers. She was smart, not afraid.

Still frowning, Sam sat down at her table and picked up a pencil. She didn't know why he'd said such a thing. But maybe he'd been joking. He had an off-kilter sense of humor that had used to make her laugh. She didn't feel like laughing now, though. The situation was too serious. Saving Brad was going to be difficult. He was more unpredictable than she remembered. Probably because he was in love. *In love.*

With a woman who didn't know the meaning of the word.

A dress took shape under the pencil. A design for Heather's wedding gown, one suited to her true personality. Sam drew white braid that circled the breasts and trimmed the full skirt in elaborate patterns. It looked like a bridal gown for an old-time saloon girl.

She sketched another design—a sheer white lace garment that stopped at the top of the thighs. With white feather trim and a matching fan, it looked like a bridal gown for a hooker. Sam studied it for a moment. No…it wasn't slutty enough for Heather.

On a fresh sheet of paper, she drew white sequined pasties, a white bikini bottom with a sheer skirt and a white feather headdress with a veil hanging down the back. Vegas showgirl bridal gown.

Sam continued to draw until she could barely hold her pencil. Finally, she went to bed, but her sleep was full of bad dreams: a seagull in a tight bronze dress swooping down and landing on Brad's shoulder. The bird started pecking at Brad's goatee and silver-rimmed sunglasses while a seagull in black matte jersey circled helplessly above, croaking pitifully, "But *I* gave him those sunglasses!"

She arrived—late—at work the next morning, entering the shop only to have an unwelcome sight meet her eyes—Heather, dressed in a golden-yellow sheath short enough to reveal every inch of her legs and tight enough to reveal the indentation of her belly button. With her boxy turquoise purse and matching ice-pick heels, she looked like an exotic butterfly next to Jeanette in her lavender suit and Kristin, Sam's sixteen-year-old sister, in jeans and T-shirt.

Heather sat enthroned at one end of the long work-table at the back of the shop while a horde of anxious handmaidens swarmed around her. Jeanette was showing her eight-by-ten glossies of wedding decorations and rattling off menu suggestions. Lin and Shin Ling, the two seamstresses whom Jeanette hired on a part-time basis, were scurrying back and forth, holding up wedding gowns and tossing bolts of cloth onto the worktable. Even Kristin was helping. She sat on Heather's other side, twisting a strand of bleached-blond hair and taking notes as Heather dictated.

And there, leaning against a wall, stood Brad, wearing khakis and a white shirt, a foam cup of coffee in his hand, looking coolly amused at the chaos.

As if sensing her presence, he glanced up. His gaze met hers, his eyes more blue than gray in the sunlit shop.

I'd be willing to bet RiversWare, my house, hell, even my car that you're still a virgin.

An indefinable emotion fluttered inside her. Confused, she glanced away, only to find Heather watching her.

"Oh, there you are, Samantha!" the blonde cooed. "How wonderful to be able to sleep in so late! But I suppose being the sister of the owner gives you certain perks. How I envy you. Being an actress, I have to be up at the crack of dawn. Not many people realize what hard work it is to make a living in Hollywood. For my *Baywatch* role, I had to report to makeup at 6:00 a.m. so they could apply instant tanning lotion. I still use it on a regular basis to keep my tan up."

Samantha saw Brad's gaze go to Heather's shoulders, covered only by the microscopic spaghetti straps of her dress. The smooth golden brown appeared perfectly natural. Sam, thinking of the many times she worked twelve-hour days—and of the orange shade her freckled, easily burnt skin had turned the time she tried an instant tanning lotion—gritted her teeth and headed for the coffee machine.

Heather didn't seem to notice Sam's lack of response. "I dragged Brad here first thing this morning," she continued. "I wanted to get started on planning our wedding right away."

"Very wise." Jeanette looked like a spinster schoolmistress next to the exotic Heather. "With only three weeks until the big day, we can't afford to waste any time."

"Three weeks!" Sam exclaimed with false dismay as she dumped a couple of tablespoons of sugar into her coffee. She had every intention of making sure that the wedding didn't take place anytime this year—or ever, for that matter. "Oh, dear, I'm sure Jeanette is too busy to plan a whole wedding in such a short time. It will take a *year,* at least. Isn't that right, Jeanette?" Sam wriggled her eyebrows at Jeanette in a significant manner.

Jeanette stared at her, a slight frown on her face, but before she could respond, Kristin piped up. "What are you talking about, Sam?" Her heavily outlined eyes looked questioningly at Sam. "Of course we can fit Brad and Heather in. This is a slow month."

Sam shot a quick glare at Kristin. Why on earth had Jeanette ever agreed to let the teenager work here? Kristin never thought before she spoke and usually managed to say exactly the wrong thing. She also wore way too much eyeliner.

"Do you think you can accommodate us?" Brad asked Jeanette.

Frowning, Jeanette hesitated, her gaze on Sam's face. "It might be difficult. There's a lot of work involved."

"And unfortunately, there's no way I could make a dress for you in three weeks." No way in *hell,* Sam added silently.

Brad glanced at Heather. "I was afraid of this, darling. I know how much you wanted a proper wedding, but as you can see, it's not possible. We're going to have to go with our original plan and get married in Las Vegas. How about tonight?"

Heather nodded. "I *told* you it didn't matter to me, sweetheart. And I really don't want to wait a whole three weeks to become your wife, anyway."

Sam burned her tongue on her coffee. They were going to get married *tonight?* She couldn't let that happen. She needed time—time to make Brad realize the mistake he was making.

"Then again," she said, backtracking as quickly as she could. "Maybe I'm being too pessimistic. Jeanette, didn't we have a cancellation yesterday? Maybe we could squeeze Brad and Heather in, after all."

"I think we could," Jeanette said woodenly.

"But what about the dress?" Brad asked.

"Really, all I have to do is design it. Lin and Shin Ling can do most of the sewing." Sam turned to the two seamstresses. "Do you think you could handle some extra sewing, ladies?"

The two women frowned grumpily. "We have lots of work already," groused Lin. She had narrow hands and could set a straight stitch that would make a plastic surgeon weep for joy.

"I don't want to get behind on my soap opera," grumbled Shin Ling. She had plump hands and could embroider in a manner that would make Leonardo da Vinci give up his paints for silk thread.

"I'll pay you triple," Brad said.

Smiles suddenly wreathing their faces, Lin and Shin Ling nodded vigorously.

"What about a church?" Kristin asked. "It will be impossible to find one at this late date."

"I'm sure we'll be able to find something," Sam said hastily, wondering why her parents hadn't drowned Kristin at birth. "There are many hotels and parks available."

Jeanette glanced at Heather. "How many people are you planning to invite?"

To Samantha's surprise, the blonde appeared a little uncertain—probably for the first time in her life, Sam thought sourly.

"We're going to have a very small wedding," Brad said. "Perhaps ten people or so."

"Ten people?" Samantha repeated. "You want us to plan a wedding and reception for ten people?"

"No, of course not," Brad corrected himself, rubbing his nose. "I meant we're going to have ten people in the wedding party. We'll want to invite a hundred or so to the ceremony."

Kristin scribbled busily on her pad. "I'll need their names and addresses so I can send out the invitations."

"And I'll need you to bring your bridesmaids and groomsmen in for fittings," Sam said reluctantly. She glanced at Brad. "Is George going to be your best man?"

"Er, no," Brad said. "I was thinking of someone else. Fred. Fred Calhoun."

Sam stared at him. "You're not asking George Yorita? But you've been friends forever. Weren't you best man at his wedding?"

"We had a bit of a falling out," Brad said.

"But you're partners!"

A dull flush rose in Brad's cheeks. "Just drop it, okay?"

"Okay," Sam said, rather stiffly.

Brad ran his fingers through his hair. "Look, Sam, I'm sorry, I didn't mean to snap."

"I understand," she said crisply. "I know weddings can put a lot of pressure on people." A *lot* of pressure.

She was feeling her own brand of pressure. She had to stop this wedding—but how? Talking to Brad hadn't worked. Trying to delay the date hadn't worked. She needed a new scheme. But what?

Brad sat down next to Heather and took her hand in his. The two sat side by side, looking at the schedule Jeanette was explaining to them, their hands tightly clasped.

Sam could barely stand to look at them. How could Brad hold Heather's hand like that? She wouldn't have thought he was the kind of guy to be so openly affectionate in public. And the way he kept looking at Heather every few seconds—it was nauseating....

The phone rang, interrupting Sam's thoughts.

Kristin picked up the phone. "Fairytale Weddings Boutique." She listened for a moment, then said, "Okay, I'll let her know." She hung up the phone and turned to Jeanette. "That was the warehouse. Our order is in."

Jeanette looked up from the schedule she and Heather were poring over. She frowned. "I need that fabric right away."

"I'll go get it," Sam volunteered. Her gaze fell on Brad and Heather's joined hands. "If Brad will come with me," she added impulsively. "I need someone to help me load the bolts."

Brad, looking oddly pleased, released Heather's hand. "Sure. I'd be glad to go with you. There are a couple things I need to talk to you about, anyway."

Samantha saw a flash of annoyance cross Heather's face. Aha! Sam thought. She'd seen similar looks on brides' faces when their fiancés tried to weasel out of going over the wedding arrangements.

Sam recognized an opportunity when she saw it. "Thanks, Brad," she said, smiling sweetly.

"But what about Heather's dress?" Kristin asked. "Shouldn't Sam get started on the design right away?"

Sam frowned at her younger sister. "I've already made some sketches."

"Well, where are they?" Kristin asked, oblivious to Sam's dark looks.

"They're in my bag." Hastily, Sam added, "I need to add a few more details."

"I'd like to see them," Brad said.

"So would I," Heather echoed him.

Sam hesitated, then went over to her bag, wondering if any of the sketches were acceptable enough to show. She pulled them out, but before she could glance through them, Brad spoke from immediately behind her.

"Oh, great," he said, tweaking the sketches from her fingers before she could stop him.

"Wait—!" But it was too late. Brad was already spreading the sketches out on the table.

For a moment, no one spoke. Everyone just stared at the drawings.

Sam bit her lip.

"Hmm, this one is interesting," Brad said, picking up a sketch of a bride in a form-fitting white leather bustier, high-rise white leather skirt, white leather dog collar and white, spike-heeled shoes. S and M bridal gown.

"Oh," Sam said weakly. "These are the wrong sketches. I must have left the ones I made for Heather at my apartment."

"But I *love* these," Heather cooed. She picked up another sketch—a skin-tight leotard with a short tulle skirt. Although the bride looked like a slutty ballerina, the dress was probably less objectionable than the others. "This one's perfect. Except the skirt should be an inch or two longer, I think."

"Fine, fine," Sam said, gathering up the sketches. Turning to Brad, she said brightly, "Now that that's all settled, can we go?"

"But doesn't Heather need Brad's help making decisions about the wedding plans?" Kristin asked.

"Heather's very good at stuff like that," Brad said. "She'd rather pick everything out herself. Wouldn't you, honey?" he said to the blonde.

Heather hesitated for a fraction of a second, then smiled brightly. "Of course. You run along, babe. I'll have oodles of fun planning our wedding."

Brad grinned. "Thanks, darling."

Sam walked out to the parking lot with Brad, wondering if he was at all aware that Heather had sounded extremely peeved at his abandonment. The longer he stayed away, the more furious the blonde was likely to be when he returned.

Sam decided to keep Brad at the warehouse as long as possible.

"It's very nice of Heather to let you come with me," Sam said, sipping her coffee as they walked across the parking lot.

"She is nice," he replied with the sublime obliviousness so common in males. "She never complains about anything."

"Not at all?" Sam raised her eyebrows. "Maybe she should apply for sainthood instead of getting married."

Brad laughed. "She's just very good-natured."

"Uh-huh," Samantha murmured, unable to keep the skepticism out of her voice.

"That's what attracted me to her—her incredible sweetness," he continued, stopping by his car. It bleeped as he turned off the alarm.

Sweet as curdled milk, Sam thought.

"She's kind…"

As a nest full of wasps.

"She's generous…"

As Ebeneezer Scrooge running the IRS.

"And she'll make the perfect wife and mother…"

As perfect as the witch in Hansel and Gretel….

Sam wondered how good-natured Heather would be after spending hours planning the thousands of details that went into a wedding. But the angrier Heather was the better, as far as Sam was concerned. With that thought in mind, all she said in response to Brad's remarks was "I'm sure she was born to drive a Suburban and take the kids to soccer games." She shook her head at his red convertible and gestured toward a boxy, three-axled delivery truck a few parking spaces away. "We'll need the van."

His gaze moved from her to the truck and back again.

"I'll drive," he said rather hastily.

She stared at him. "Why?"

"I've gotten used to it. Heather doesn't drive. She's from Ohio and she's afraid of the freeways."

Could the blonde do anything useful? Sam wondered. "That sounds like a pain in the neck."

"Not at all. I don't mind."

"It makes her so dependent on you, though." To demonstrate how *in*dependent women behaved, she said, "You don't need to drive. I'm a native and the freeways don't scare *me*."

Brad rubbed the back of his neck. "I know they don't, but well, to be perfectly truthful, you're a terrible driver."

"What!"

Gently, he plucked the keys from her fingers and opened the passenger door for her. "You heard me."

"You're crazy," she said as she automatically stepped up into the truck. "I've never even gotten a ticket!"

Brad walked around to the driver's side and climbed in. "Only because you talk your way out of them. No officer can resist those big green-and-gold eyes of yours."

Sam sat stiffly in her seat, holding her cup of coffee as he started the engine and shifted into gear. The truck chugged as it warmed up. He shifted gears again as he pulled onto the street and headed for the on-ramp.

Once they were on the freeway, he asked, "Are you mad at me?"

She set her cup of coffee on the dashboard, maintaining a dignified silence.

"Come on, Sam. You know it's the truth."

"It most certainly is not!" She'd never been very good at maintaining a dignified silence. "I can't believe you would be so rude."

He smiled wryly. "I think that's what my problem was with you. I was always too polite. And you never could admit the truth."

The truth? She glared at his profile. What was he talking about? She opened her mouth to ask, then paused. She looked down at the seat. The vinyl had split open and gray stuffing was coming out. She could buy some upholstery tape to repair it. But the seat would always have the ugly patch on it.

"It's good to be polite," she said instead.

His smile turned enigmatic; he made no reply.

"Besides," she continued, "I don't know how you can say I'm a terrible driver. You taught me to drive."

To her relief, he laughed. "One of my worst failures."

"So, what did you want to talk to me about?" she asked, rolling up the window to block out the noise and the hot, smoggy air.

He shot her a quick glance before checking the side mirror and changing lanes. "Vera called me last night."

"Oh?" Sam's fingers tightened on the edge of her seat. Her mother always meant well, but... "What did she want?"

"Well, it seems news travels fast—she heard that

I got engaged. Vera said she wanted to assure me that she still considers me part of the family." He applied pressure to the brakes as the traffic in front of him slowed. "And that Heather and I would always be welcome in her home."

Brad had always spent the holidays at her parents' house. But Brad and *Heather?* A vision of the two of them dropping in at Christmas filled Sam's head. She shuddered. Of course, things wouldn't go that far; Sam planned to break up the engagement long before then. But if she failed...

What on earth was her mother thinking of? "Do you plan to take her up on that?" Sam asked.

"I don't know. Is it okay with you, Sam?"

Sam picked up her coffee and sipped it, trying to think of a reason to say no. She wanted to say that no way was she going to spend so much as the Firemen's Pancake Breakfast with Heather. But if worse came to worst, and the two of them actually got married, could she exclude Brad? She remembered how Easter had been without him—the day had seemed flat and gray.

"Of course it's okay with me," she heard herself say.

Brad heaved a loud sigh of relief. "That's settled, then. I'm hoping you and Heather will become good friends. She likes you a lot, Sam. In fact, she wants you to be her maid-of-honor."

Involuntarily, Sam's hand jerked, causing her to spill hot coffee all over herself. "Oow!"

Brad glanced over at her. "Are you okay?"

"Yeah." She looked in the glove box and found some napkins. She dabbed at her jeans.

"So, will you do the maid-of-honor thing?"

"Um…" The boxy interior of the truck was very warm. Sam rolled down the window and inhaled diesel fumes as she tried to think of some excuse. "Doesn't she have any friends? Or a sister or something?"

"No. I told you, the women here haven't been very friendly. She doesn't know very many people. She's an only child and her parents are both dead."

Sam bit her lip. She disliked Heather and didn't want to feel any sympathy for her. But in spite of herself, she couldn't help feeling a twinge. Having lost her own father, she knew how hard losing a parent was.

"C'mon, Sam. You've always said I'm your best friend. I need you to help Heather out on this."

Sam didn't want to help Heather. But she couldn't refuse Brad, either. Reluctantly, she said, "If you're sure that's what Heather wants."

"Oh, I'm sure," Brad said, a smile in his voice.

Sam was glad when they arrived at the warehouse almost an hour later. Inside, hundreds of bolts of fabric were piled haphazardly on shelves, tables and even the floor. The room was long and narrow, with ugly beige walls, a concrete floor and high windows, but Sam paid no attention to the dreary surroundings. All her attention was focused on the cornucopia before her: chintz, denim, chambray, tweed and gabardine. Luscious cashmeres and creamy leathers. Dotted swiss satin and chartreuse taffeta and rhinestone-studded gauze.

Her troubles momentarily forgotten, Sam moved from table to table, inspecting the bolts and testing the weave of the various fabrics while a salesclerk searched the stockroom for Jeanette's order.

She glanced up once to see Brad watching her, a rather odd smile on his face.

"What?" she asked.

"Nothing," he said. "I was just remembering that time I took you to the homecoming dance."

Sam remembered the occasion—it had been her senior year and she'd just broken up with Sean Chang. Determined to go to the dance anyway, she'd asked Brad if he would drive her to the school. He'd agreed, and even hung around to talk to one of his old teachers who was chaperoning the dance.

"Yeah, what about it?" she asked.

"You had to work late that night. I picked you up at that fabric store where you worked, but you'd forgotten your dress, so you wrapped yourself in a piece of gold silk and knotted it together."

"Oh, yes, I remember," she said. "The silk kept getting caught on your belt buckle, that one dance." She'd apologized, but he hadn't seemed too upset. "I'm surprised you even remember that."

"Oh, I remember, all right. I could see that knot you'd tied right between your breasts. All night I kept wondering what would happen if I untied it."

"I would have killed you, that's what would have happened," she said, laughing a little. "If I remember correctly, that particular knot was holding the dress together. If you'd untied it, the whole thing would have fallen apart. I had barely anything on underneath, either."

"Hmm. I thought you didn't."

Something in his voice made her look at him. He wasn't looking at her, however. He was staring down at a bolt of silk, his fingers caressing the cloth gently.

An image rose in her mind of the two of them

dancing, and his hand resting on her bare back. She had been aware of his touch without thinking too much about it. It had been a pleasant sensation, the slight roughness of his fingers warm against her skin. It had seemed perfectly innocent....

She glanced away, a flush warming her skin. "I'm finished," she said abruptly, embarrassed by her train of thought. It *had* been innocent. "Let's go."

The salesclerk rang up the order and Brad helped Sam load the truck. Within half an hour, they were on their way back to the shop.

Brad was silent during the drive, and Sam was too involved with her own thoughts to try to draw him out. She couldn't stop thinking about what he'd said about untying the knot in her dress. She remembered seeing him every once in a while that evening; he'd been standing at the sidelines, watching her dance with various boys. She'd smiled whenever she saw him, but he hadn't smiled back. On the drive back home he'd been quiet—very quiet. That whole evening had been peculiar; almost as peculiar as his comment about her dress. The remark had an almost...*sexual* overtone to it.

But no, she must be imagining it. The Brad she'd known would never think erotic thoughts about her. Probably the only thing he'd ever fantasized about were computers—he'd been obsessed with them. She couldn't imagine him having a lustful thought back then. Maybe now...she glanced at him sideways. His eyes were fixed on the road, throwing his profile into relief. His nose was slightly aquiline, his lips firm, his chin...

She hurried past his chin to his neck, not thick like a football player's, but sturdy and strong all the same, and down to muscular forearms revealed by the rolled-up sleeves of his shirt. His hands on the steering wheel were steady, confident. They were the hands of an experienced man, a man who knew exactly what he was doing....

Sam turned her gaze away and looked out her window, not really seeing the other cars. Brad was engaged. He must be thinking lustful thoughts now. The way he looked at Heather, he obviously *was*. Sometimes he looked like the Wolf, smacking his lips, waiting for Little Red Riding Hood to get close enough to eat.

But at other times, his gaze was gentle, tender, with a smile in his eyes that made something in her stomach tighten. She hated it when he looked at Heather like that. The blonde didn't deserve to be looked at like that.

"I wonder how Heather is doing," Sam said a while later as they pulled into the shop's parking lot. "She might be a little miffed that you left her alone so long." Or a *lot* miffed, if Sam was lucky.

Brad appeared unconcerned as they climbed down from the truck and walked across the parking lot toward the shop. "I'm sure she's fine. Jeanette and Kristin will have helped her if she had any problems."

If Jeanette and Kristin hadn't murdered the bitchy blonde. Jeanette was usually very good with difficult clients, but even her patience had limits. As for Kristin—the teenager had an unfortunate tendency to say exactly what she was thinking.

By now, the tension among the women would be thick, Sam thought. Brad would have to notice it.

Even if he didn't, she could count on Kristin to bluntly state her opinion of his fiancée.

Maybe, if Sam was really lucky, the women would actually be fighting. Brad would see Heather's true personality for himself. Sam paused at the door, listening hopefully for screams, shouts or thumps.

"What are you doing?" Brad asked.

"Oh…nothing." Holding her breath, Sam eased the door open.

The three women sitting on the sofa looked around. They were all smiling.

"Brad!" Heather jumped to her feet and ran over to hug him. "I missed you!"

"I missed you, too, honey," he said fondly.

"We've only been gone a few hours," Sam pointed out, trying to hide her disappointment at Heather's happy greeting.

"Was that all? It seemed like an eternity. But we got a lot done while you were gone." Heather tucked her arm through Brad's and beamed up at him. "We've sent out five hundred invitations."

"Five hundred!" For a moment, Brad lost his smile. "I'm surprised you know that many people, sweetheart."

"Well, half of them are your employees, of course."

Brad looked as though he'd swallowed a lemon. "You invited everyone at RiversWare?"

"Certainly. I called your secretary and explained and she downloaded the whole address database. And Kristin is a whiz with computers—she printed up the invitations and envelopes in no time at all."

"Maybe I better look at them…just to make sure

you didn't miss anyone," Brad said. "Where are they?"

"The mailman just took them," Jeanette said. "But you can check the database list."

"I'll have my secretary go over it," Brad muttered.

"Brad, wait until you see the menu!" Kristin enthused. "Caviar and truffles and the best champagne! And the luckiest thing—we were able to book the temple Heather wanted."

"The temple?" Brad said rather blankly.

"The Temple of Peace and Tranquility. Heather went to a wedding there a couple of months ago and she said it's been her dream ever since to be married there. They had a cancellation, so we were able to squeeze you in."

"I knew you would want the best," Heather said sweetly.

Brad stared at his fiancée, and Sam found herself holding her breath again. Clearly he was not pleased by Heather's lavish arrangements—and no wonder. It was going to cost him a fortune. Was he finally seeing Heather for what she was—a greedy, selfish woman who cared only about his money?

Brad burst into laughter. "Of course I want the best. What about the reception?"

"We reserved a lovely hotel by the beach," Heather said. "We even reserved the honeymoon suite there for our wedding night."

"Excellent," Brad said, still laughing. "But I think I'd better take you back to your hotel before you bankrupt me. Bye, everyone." He hustled Heather out of the shop.

Frowning, Sam watched them go. Brad was much too nice; he'd let Heather off much too easily. It was obvious the blonde had taken advantage of Brad's absence to spend as much of his money as she possibly could. Poor Brad. How could he be so blind?

She turned to her sisters. Jeanette stood in the middle of the room, arms folded across her chest, her toe tapping like a disapproving schoolteacher's. Kristin, her hazel eyes half concealed by the strand of bleached blond hair hanging in her face, stared at her curiously.

Sam knew immediately what was wrong. "I'm sorry I left you two alone with Heather," she said apologetically.

Jeanette's toe stopped tapping. "What are you talking about?" she burst out. "What the heck were you doing? Are you trying to ruin my business? I almost fainted when I saw those sketches. Thank God Heather is such a nice woman. I'm surprised she didn't walk out the door."

Sam's mouth fell open. "Didn't you find her...difficult to work with?"

"Not at all," Jeanette snapped.

Kristin picked up a pattern book and shoved it onto the shelf. "What are you talking about, Sam? She had a lot of really cool ideas."

"She was very pleasant," Jeanette said, a little more calmly. "I confess, I had my doubts when I heard Brad was marrying an actress, but I must say I liked her. She wants Cassie to be her flower girl."

"Oh, does she?" Sam could hardly believe her ears. Heather must have decided to play the part of the perfect fiancée for her sisters. The blonde had even discovered Jeanette's soft spot—her children. Cassie would adore being a flower girl. Sam couldn't believe that Jeanette had fallen for Heather's act. Jeanette was usually very perceptive about people.

"She's perfect for Brad," Kristin added.

"No, she's not!" Sam burst out.

Jeanette and Kristin stared at her as though she'd lost her mind.

"I know Heather can be charming," Sam hastily explained. "I was fooled at first also. But the truth of the matter is, she is a terrible, horrible person. Last night at the restaurant, when we were in the rest room together, she as good as admitted that she didn't love Brad, that she was only marrying him for his money. She says she's not going to let him give anything to his employees, that she's going to get him to use it to finance a movie that she'll star in, she hates kids and she *smokes!* Poor Brad. He has no idea. She's taking advantage of his trusting nature."

Her sisters regarded her rather doubtfully.

"Lots of my friends smoke." Kristin pushed the strand of hair out of her face. It stayed in place for a second before flopping back down. "It's stupid, but it doesn't mean they're evil."

"Brad's trusting nature?" Jeanette repeated. "I've always thought he was pretty shrewd, myself. I doubt anyone could trick him—at least, not for very long."

"Heather is very slick," Sam said.

"Not so slick if she told you all this about herself," Kristin pointed out. "Why would she do that?"

"I don't know." Sam frowned a little. "Maybe because I caught her off guard in the rest room. I saw her smoking so she knew I wouldn't be fooled by her act much longer. Or maybe because she's incredibly arrogant. But it doesn't really matter. The important thing is that Brad doesn't stand a chance against her!"

"Maybe he doesn't want a chance against her," Jeanette said.

"Believe me, he will when he finds out what she's really like. She will make him miserable. She's already trying to change him. She bought him new clothes and forced him to eat stuff like jicama!"

"Sounds like an improvement to me." Jeanette sat down at the worktable and started making notes on a large pad.

"*Looks* like an improvement, too," Kristin added. "I never realized how sexy Brad is."

Sam stared at her little sister in disbelief. "Sexy?"

"Yeah, sexy. He has a sort of intense aura about him. I never noticed it before. Like if he sees something he wants, he'll go after it and keep after it until he gets it, no matter what he has to do, no matter how long it takes—"

Sam snorted. "What are you talking about? Brad is the most easygoing guy around. Where do you get these weird ideas? Never mind," she added hastily as Kristin opened her mouth to respond. "Whatever he looks like, Brad is our friend and we must stop him from marrying Heather."

There was a small silence.

"I don't think it's really our business." Jeanette scribbled a note on her pad.

"Brad's a grown man—it's not like we can tell him what to do," Kristin agreed, picking up a thick catalog from the table.

Sam glared at her sisters. "I think it's our duty as his friends to tell him the truth about Heather."

"I don't think he would believe you," Kristin said. "I'm not sure *I* believe you."

"Oh, for heaven's sake, why would I lie?"

Jeanette and Kristin exchanged glances.

"Sam," Jeanette said in a soothing voice that sounded a lot like their mother's, "you aren't…jealous, are you?"

"Jealous!" Sam sighed in frustration. "Of course not! I'm only trying to help Brad!"

"Okay, okay, if you say so," Jeanette said. "So I take it you *are* going to say something to him about Heather?"

"I already tried," Sam admitted. "But he's blind when it comes to her. So I must find some other way to break up their engagement."

"Maybe if you told *her* something horrible about Brad, she wouldn't want to marry him," Kristin suggested.

Sam tried to think of something horrible about Brad, but nothing occurred to her. "Like what?"

"Maybe how selfish husbands are," Jeanette said. "How they expect their wives to do everything."

Sam eyed Jeanette uneasily. Apparently the marriage counseling sessions weren't going so well. "I don't think Brad is like that."

"You could tell her he snores," Kristin suggested.

Paying no attention to Kristin, Jeanette continued broodingly, "All men are like that. They're complete slobs who expect you to fix their dinner, then wash the dishes and clean up while they sit in front of the TV—"

"Maybe you could tell her that he has a problem with gas," Kristin advised.

Sam ignored her younger sister also. "Brad always helps clean up at holiday meals," she told Jeanette.

Jeanette wasn't listening. "And *then*," she said bitterly, "after working and taking care of three kids all day long, when you're completely exhausted and just want to go to sleep, *then* they want to have *sex*—''

''I know!'' Kristin said brightly. ''We could say that Brad is a premature ejaculator—''

Sam choked.

''Kristin!'' Jeanette pokered up like a Victorian spinster.

''What?'' Kristin looked surprised.

''What do you know about premature ejaculators?'' Sam asked.

Kristin rolled her eyes. ''I read 'Dear Abby.'''

''Mother would have a fit if she heard you talking like that!'' Jeanette scolded.

''I'm not an idiot,'' Kristin said indignantly. ''I know better than to talk about sex in front of Mom.'' Her brows drew together a little. ''Actually, the premature-ejaculator thing may not be such a good idea. Heather probably already knows that Brad isn't one. They've probably made love hundreds of times. In hundreds of places. In hundreds of ways—''

''Kristin!'' This time it was Sam, fighting an urge to clap a hand over Kristin's mouth, who protested.

''What?'' Kristin looked disgusted. ''What's with you? I know you're a prude when it comes to sex, but you can't expect the rest of us to be the same.''

''I'm not a prude,'' Sam said, defending herself. ''I have morals. And anyway, Brad and Heather are not sleeping together.''

''Uh-huh,'' Kristin said, her disbelief plain. Even Jeanette looked skeptical.

''It's true,'' Sam insisted. ''Brad told me himself. Heather wants to wait for the wedding night.''

''Well, I don't think she's going to hold out much longer. Did you see the way she looked at him? I'll bet she's been having some pretty hot fantasies. Like—''

"Never mind," Sam said quickly.

Jeanette frowned at the sixteen year old. "You're too young to be talking like that."

Kristin snorted and opened her mouth to reply.

"Can't you think of some other way to break Brad and Heather up?" Sam asked before a fight erupted.

"I don't see *you* coming up with any brilliant ideas," Kristin grumbled. But then her expression brightened. "I know! You said Heather hates kids, right? Well, maybe if you take her somewhere where there are lots of kids, she'll have a fit."

"I doubt she'd have a fit just because she saw a few kids," Sam said.

"Yeah, she'd have to be directly involved with them somehow," Jeanette agreed.

"Hey, I know!" Kristin said. "How about if we get her and Brad to baby-sit Jeanette's kids!"

Sam perked up. "That might work...if anyone could make Heather lose her cool, it would be Audrey, Brendan and Cassie."

Jeanette stiffened. "What's that supposed to mean?"

"Oh, nothing," Sam told her. "You know I love your kids. But even you have to admit that they can be a little bit trying at times."

"My children are angels!"

"I don't know if I'd call them angels, Jeanette," Kristin said doubtfully. "They may *look* like angels, but they act like little demons. Sweet demons," she added hastily, seeing Jeanette's face.

Jeanette's expression remained stiff.

"Your kids are perfect," Sam said. Jeanette's expression softened.

"At least for what I have in mind," Sam added.

Jeanette started to stiffen up again, but then she laughed. "You two are terrible. At least I know where my kids got their fiendish personalities."

"You're blaming us?" Sam asked. "What about that husband of yours?"

"Well…he might have contributed something," Jeanette admitted. "Okay, I'll allow my kids to be used for Brad's sake—if he'll agree to take them."

"That should be no problem," Sam said grimly, "since Mom has told him to consider himself 'one of the family' and he's taken her up on it. There's no reason we can't ask him to baby-sit tomorrow."

"Tomorrow is Wednesday," Kristin pointed out. "Brad's not going to want to take a day off work to baby-sit."

Unfortunately, Kristin was probably right. "Saturday, then."

"You really think he'll do it?" Jeanette asked.

"Sure, why not? He loves your kids."

In spite of her words, Sam wasn't quite so confident as she sounded. Brad was bound to think her request rather strange.

She glanced at her watch. He'd had enough time to drop Heather at her hotel, but not enough to reach his house in San Clemente. She went into Jeanette's little office and dialed the cell phone number he'd left with Jeanette.

There was no answer. She put down the phone, frowning. Then, slowly, she picked it up again and dialed Heather's hotel. When she was connected to Heather's room, Brad answered.

"Hello?"

Something twisted inside Sam's stomach. *They've probably made love in hundreds of places, in hundreds of ways....*

"Hello?" Brad said again.

Sam shook off her unpleasant thoughts. "Hi, Brad," she said brightly. "I was calling because I wondered if you could do me a favor."

"Sure. What?"

"Mom just called to tell Jeanette that she can't watch the kids on Saturday, and we wondered if maybe you and Heather would mind taking them."

Silence.

"You want me to baby-sit your sister's kids?" he finally said.

"Yes, well, I wouldn't usually ask it, but there's a big wedding Saturday night, and we're having to do a lot of extra work to arrange yours on such short notice, and you *did* say you wanted to see them."

"Yeah, I did, but I don't know anything about baby-sitting."

"Oh, I'm sure Heather will help you. She loves kids, doesn't she?"

"Yes, but—"

"Then it's settled," Sam interrupted, afraid that he was going to refuse. "Can you pick them up here about 10:00 a.m. on Saturday?"

There was another long silence. Sam pressed her knuckles against her mouth, praying that he would say yes. The problem with Brad was that it was difficult to know what he was thinking. Normally very easygoing, he could dig his heels in at the most unexpected times. Usually when she had done something particularly outrageous. So maybe this request was a little outrageous. But it was all in a good cause—saving him from Heather.

"Okay."

Sam let out a long sigh of relief. "Thanks, Brad. We really appreciate it."

"I'm sure you do. See you Saturday."

Chapter Five

The first thing Sam heard when she opened the door to the shop Saturday morning was crying.

"I don't want to go-o-o-o with them!" she heard a small voice wail.

Foreboding filling her, she entered the shop to find five-year-old Cassie clinging to Jeanette's legs. Brendan, age six, was running around the worktable, his little legs churning like pistons. Audrey, all of eight years old, gazed dreamily out the window.

Sam stole a glance at Brad. He looked amused, she was relieved to see. Heather, on the other hand, was clicking her long, French-manicured nails on the counter by the cash register. Her mouth was pursed just the tiniest bit, and the expression in her eyes as she gazed at the three children was decidedly cool.

Her plan really might work, Sam thought in delight. "Good morning!" she said loudly so as to be heard over Cassie's sobs.

Cassie abruptly stopped screaming. "Hi, Aunt Sama'tha," she lisped.

"What's wrong, Cassie?" Sam knelt beside the child and put an arm around her.

Cassie's big brown eyes filled with tears again.

"We have a small problem," Brad intervened. "Cassie doesn't want to go with us."

"If Cassie's not going, I'm not going, either," Audrey said.

"I'll go!" Brendan shouted, not pausing in his minimarathon.

"If your sisters don't go, you're not going, either," Jeanette informed her son.

Sam groaned silently. Her perfect plan…ruined! Unless she did something—fast. "Cassie, don't you want to go with Brad?" she said coaxingly. "He's going to take you someplace fun."

Cassie's out-thrust lower lip trembled. "Where?"

"Where would you like to go?" Brad asked promptly.

"To the maze!" Brendan leapt over a pile of magazines on the floor.

"Oh, the *maze!*" Sam said. "The maze is *lots* of fun. It's my absolute *favorite* place to go. Wouldn't you like to go there, Cassie?"

Cassie sucked her thumb while she considered. Samantha held her breath. "Come on, Cassie, you don't want to miss the *maze.*"

Cassie took her thumb out of her mouth. "Okay, I'll go…if you come, too, Aunt Sama'tha."

"Me!" Sam rocked back on her heels. "Oh, sweetie, I can't. I have lots of work to do—"

"Then I'm not going, either," Cassie said mulishly. "I'll stay and help you with your work. Mommy says I'm a wunnerful helper."

Sam barely repressed a shudder. She looked at Jeanette, but Jeanette just shrugged.

Sam considered her options: go or give up her plan. She glanced at Heather.

The blonde still watched the children—was that a hint of distaste curling her mouth?

Sam made her decision. "Okay, I'll go with you."

Cassie smiled radiantly. Brad smiled, too. Heather arched her brows.

"I thought you had to work on some big wedding for tonight," the blonde said.

"As long as I'm back by five o'clock, it'll be fine," Sam said.

"If you're not going to work, then there's really no need for Brad and me to watch the children," Heather pointed out with irritating logic.

"Oh, but…but the kids will be so disappointed if you don't go!"

"I don't care if they come or not," Brendan shouted.

"Brendan!" Jeanette remonstrated. "That's very rude."

"Oh. Sorry." Brendan kept running.

"I'm sure you'll want to spend some time with them, Heather," Sam said. "Especially Cassie, since she's going to be in your wedding."

"I want to go," Brad said to his fiancée. "Is it all right with you, darling? I'd like to take the kids out. I haven't seen them in a long time."

Heather didn't look too happy, but she nodded grudgingly.

The matter settled, they all piled into Brad's car—

he was driving a Jeep Cherokee today—and headed for the maze. Since there were only five seat belts, Sam ended up in the back with Cassie on her lap. The kids bounced and shouted and sang, but Sam didn't quiet them as she usually would have. The more racket to grate on Heather's nerves, the better, Sam thought—even though her own head was beginning to pound.

They arrived at the maze and Brad bought the tickets.

"Must we really do this?" Sam heard Heather say in an undertone to Brad. To hide her gleeful smile, Sam bent down to tie Cassie's shoe.

"We can't disappoint the kids," Brad said, nudging the blonde forward.

The maze was a series of plywood walls with towers at periodic points. The object was to find each of the towers and use the hole-punchers there to cut the letters *M-A-Z-E* on a card, then find the way out again. The one who finished in the fastest time was the winner.

The three adults each took one of the children. Heather eyed Brendan, who was butting his head against the maze wall, and Cassie, who was talking nonstop. She quickly grabbed Audrey's hand and entered the maze.

Sam smiled again. Audrey might seem sweet and dreamy, but she was as strong and athletic as a little horse. She would run Heather ragged.

Brad put his hand on Brendan's shoulder and said, "We men need to stick together, right, Brendan?"

"Yeah!" Brendan shouted. "Come on, let's go!"

They disappeared into the maze.

"Are you going with me, Aunt Sama'tha?" Cassie asked.

Sam gazed down into Cassie's luminous brown eyes, then looked at the maze. "Wouldn't you rather stay out here?" she asked hopefully.

Cassie shook her head vigorously, causing her short dark brown hair to swing. "Audrey and Brendan got to go. I wanna go, too."

Knowing she had no chance of changing Cassie's mind, Sam took the little girl's hand and reluctantly entered the maze.

An hour later, Sam was sorry she'd ever come up with this plan. Why did Brendan have to pick going to the maze? Why couldn't he have chosen Disneyland or Knott's Berry Farm or even the beach like a normal child? She and Cassie had not found a single tower and were hopelessly lost in the middle of the maze. Cassie, who had started out running, was now exhausted. "I'm tired of this," she whined. "Let's go home."

"We have to find the exit first, sweetie," Sam said, trying to smile. She wasn't sure she'd ever make it out. She'd come with a group of kids in high school once and spent hours running like a mouse through the endless corridors. She'd sworn at the time never to come here again. How could she have forgotten that vow? she wondered as they turned another corner...and ran smack-dab into Brad's hard chest.

His arms came up immediately to steady her.

"Hi, beautiful," he said, smiling down at her.

Sam stood there, staring up into his eyes, her heart giving an odd, sharp thump.

"We've found the *M* and the *Z*," Brendan boasted. "Have you found any yet, Cassie?"

Cassie's lower lip started to tremble.

"We're still looking," Sam said hastily, stepping away from Brad. "Cassie is helping me a lot. I don't think I would have gotten this far without her."

"Come back this way, Cassie," Brad said kindly, taking the child's hand. He led them to the left, to the right and then to the right again, and there was one of the towers.

"Brendan, take Cassie up and help her punch her card," Brad said.

"Aw, do I have to?" Brendan asked.

"Yes," Brad said.

Brad's voice was sufficiently firm that Brendan obeyed without any further argument. Brad turned to Sam. "Having fun?"

"Whoever invented this place ought to be shot," she retorted, leaning wearily against the plywood wall.

He laughed. "How can you say that? Remember that time we came here in high school?"

"Yeah, I remember, all right. I broke up with Pete Mitchell a second time because he abandoned me in the middle of this place." Sam shuddered a little. She'd unwisely worn a miniskirt and pointy-toed high heels, and within minutes of entering the maze, she'd had blisters on all ten of her toes. Pete, whom she'd foolishly decided to give a second chance, had grown impatient with her mincing steps and taken off. Having no sense of direction, she'd been fighting a rising panic as she limped through the poorly lit maze, when a shadow loomed up behind her. She'd turned, her heart pounding, a scream welling up in her throat...

Only to find Brad standing there, a frown knitting his forehead.

He wore much the same expression now.

"Mitchell was a jerk," Brad muttered.

Sam nodded. "If you hadn't found me, I would have been lost forever."

He smiled at her melodramatic statement. "You should have known I would find you." He pushed a damp strand of hair back from her forehead, then put his hand against the wall by her head.

She smiled up at him. "I was never so happy to see anyone in my life. I could have kissed you."

"Hmm, you should have gone right ahead. I wouldn't have objected."

She laughed. "I'll bet you would have. I was like a sister to you—you would have died of embarrassment."

"You think so?"

Something in his voice made her glance at him. He was still smiling, but there was an odd expression in his level gaze. Inexplicably, Sam's heart gave another of those peculiar sharp thumps. Why was he looking at her like that? As if he was waiting for something. Something from her.

She looked toward the steps of the tower. "I broke up with Pete the next day. I remember I was delighted because it looked like someone had punched him in the face."

"He deserved it," Brad murmured.

Sam frowned a little at the words. "You didn't... no, never mind." The thought was ridiculous.

"Didn't what? Punch his daylights out? Of course I did."

She gaped at him. "But...but how could you beat

up Pete? He must have outweighed you by fifty pounds.''

''The school I'd come from was a lot different—you learned to take care of yourself. You think I couldn't take a soft beach boy from Santa Monica?''

His voice was cool and amused, but her eyes were drawn to the angle of his chin. *That chin!* Sam put the palms of her hands against the plywood wall behind her. ''But *why* would you beat him up?''

''Why do you think, Sam?''

A slight smile curved his mouth as he looked down at her. He was standing very close, she realized suddenly. Had he moved? She wasn't sure. She just knew that his outstretched arm was brushing her shoulder, that the pupils of his eyes looked very dark against the blue rim of his irises, that the smile on his mouth was fading....

''We did it, Aunt Sama'tha!''

Brad stepped back, his arm dropping to his side. Sam, feeling strangely hot and bothered, forced herself to turn and smile at her niece.

''Are you all right, Aunt Sama'tha?'' Cassie asked, staring at her curiously. ''Your face is all red.''

The heat in Sam's face increased. ''I'm fine,'' she said as she stepped away from the wall. ''Let me see the card.''

Cassie, easily distracted, held up the card with a big grin. The *M* was rather mutilated from the hole punch.

''Good job, Cassie. Come on, we'd better go look for those other letters.''

She started to turn away, but Brad's hand on her arm stopped her. Startled, she looked at it, then up at him.

"Wait." He was staring at her with that watchful gaze. "Maybe we should join forces. We can search the rest of the maze together."

Her skin felt warm where he was touching her. Uncomfortably warm. "I don't think so—"

"Uncle Brad!" Brendan protested vociferously. "They're *girls*. They'll slow us down."

Sam smiled brightly. "Brendan's right. C'mon, Cassie. Let's go."

But Sam couldn't go, because Brad was still holding her arm, his eyes narrowing down at her. "Running away again, Sam?"

"I don't know what you're talking about." But she couldn't quite meet his gaze.

"Uh-huh." Brad released her arm and stepped back, his voice cool. "Go ahead and run, Sammy. While you still can."

She almost did. She walked quickly, Cassie skipping along at her side. Not until they turned a corner did her steps and heartbeat slow down a fraction. Confused, more disoriented than ever, she let Cassie lead the way, trying to figure out what had just happened.

She wasn't very successful. An image kept replaying in her head of Brad's fist plowing into Pete's face.

What had possessed him? Why had he done it?

Why do you think? he'd said.

Out of some misguided sense of responsibility, she supposed. Her mother had asked him to look out for her, which Sam had thought totally ridiculous, and she'd told him so. He'd grinned and nodded, but he'd often lurked in the background. She'd been more concerned about *him*—new to the school, quiet and distant. After the incident with Pete picking on him, she'd given herself the task of shielding him from bullies.

Only now it appeared he hadn't really needed protection.

He'd been taller than Pete, but leaner. It wasn't that Brad had looked weak, but that Pete had a reputation for being a brawler. She'd known Brad had come from an inner-city school, but she hadn't thought he was a fighter.

She'd thought she knew him so well. Now she wondered if she'd known him at all. She always thought of Brad as an easygoing guy. And usually he was. But in spite of what she'd said to Kristin, she'd always been aware of an undercurrent to him. He didn't talk about his feelings much, but he could be— what had Kristin called it?—*intense* in a way that had sometimes made her uneasy....

"Aunt Sama'tha, look!" Cassie cried. "The exit!"

Sam followed Cassie through the turnstile, only to stop short as she saw Heather sitting on a bench while Audrey played in the postage-stamp-size playground.

"Ah, there you are," Heather said coolly. "I was beginning to wonder if something had happened to you and Brad."

A wave of heat warmed Sam's face again. She fanned herself with the maze ticket, hoping her cheeks weren't as red as they felt.

Audrey came running over, saving Sam from having to reply. "We found all the letters and finished in thirty minutes!" she boasted. "Heather didn't get lost once!"

Audrey proudly held up her card, showing neatly punched letters and the time clearly stamped, proving that they had indeed spent a mere thirty minutes and twenty-three seconds in the maze.

Sam looked at Heather in disbelief.

The blonde's mouth curled in a feline smile. "I know the secret."

Hot and sticky after her ordeal in the maze, Sam hated Heather more than ever. With anyone else, she would have asked what the secret was, but she couldn't bring herself to admit that she didn't know— even though it was perfectly obvious she didn't.

Cassie had no such proud inhibitions. "What is it? What is it?" she cried, jumping up and down.

Heather shook her head. "I can't tell. You have to discover it for yourself."

She sounded like something out of a *Star Wars* movie, Sam thought in disgust. And why was the woman staring at her that way?

Brad and Brendan came out of the maze, distracting Heather. Sam, her cheeks heating up again, couldn't quite look at Brad.

Stop it, she told herself. *You're being ridiculous.*

Taking a deep breath, she looked directly at him.

He wasn't even paying any attention to her. He was crouched beside Audrey, admiring her card. "Heather knows the secret," the little girl announced solemnly.

Brad arched an eyebrow and stood up, gazing at Heather with respect. He put his arm around her and whispered in her ear.

Samantha's hands clenched into fists. She'd thought something had happened in the maze. She'd thought...she'd thought she'd seen something in his eyes. But obviously she must have imagined it. Brad couldn't take his eyes—or his hands—off the blonde.

Sam felt curiously flat. Her plan to make Heather

reveal her dislike of children had failed miserably, and no wonder. Heather had all the advantages— beauty, cleverness and the Secret. Brad might not need protection from the Petes of this world, but he was no match for the Heathers. He might seem cool to some, but she knew that his feelings ran deep. When he'd told her about his parents' and sister's deaths, his words had been rough, terse. He hadn't cried, but there had been a look in his eyes, a rawness, that made the tears well up in her own eyes and run down her cheeks.

Even now, the memory of that look made her throat feel tight. No one should ever have to look like that. Especially not Brad. Especially not because of someone like Heather. Sam had to do something to extricate him from the blonde's French-manicured claws. But what?

The question gnawed at her on the drive back to the shop. She sat in the back seat, Cassie on her lap, trying to think of some new plan while the kids sang "One Hundred and One Bottles of Milk on the Wall."

"Samantha," Brad said at seventy-two bottles, raising his voice to be heard over the children's singing. "I have a surprise for you."

"A surprise?" The car went over a dip in the road and her stomach did a little somersault.

Brad, his gaze on the traffic, nodded. "Heather has organized a charity in-line skating race for tomorrow—I signed you up to participate."

The car bounced again, more roughly this time, going over a pothole. Sam clutched the armrest. "You did what?"

"I signed you up to skate in the in-line skating

race.'' Brad glanced quickly over his shoulder to smile at her. ''It's for a worthy cause.''

''But I can't...'' Sam stopped abruptly. *I can't skate,* she'd been about to say. But she'd told Brad and Heather she could.

''I'm really sorry,'' she lied glibly. ''But I'm busy tomorrow. There's a big wedding.''

''On Sunday?'' Heather asked.

''The bride and groom are Jewish,'' Sam said.

''You're confused,'' Brad said. ''The Feldman wedding is *next* Sunday. I already talked to Jeanette and she said she didn't need you tomorrow.''

''But I need to work on Heather's dress. I'm already behind. And I need to come up with something for the bridesmaid dresses—''

''That's all taken care of,'' Brad said. ''Heather chose the bridesmaid dresses this morning.''

Sam looked warily at the back of the blonde's perfectly coiffed head. ''Heather picked out a dress for me?''

''I helped!'' Cassie chirped. ''It's *beautiful,* Aunt Sama'tha. With lots of pink ruffles.''

Seeing the smirk on Heather's lips, Sam almost said the only time she'd wear pink ruffles was to a certain blonde's funeral, but she managed to restrain herself. At least the dress gave her an excuse to avoid the race. ''I'll need to be fitted and start on the sewing—''

''Shin Ling said she has your measurements,'' Brad said. ''She and Lin are going to do the sewing. They said their families could really use the extra money.''

Sam tried to keep the desperation out of her voice. ''I'll probably be too tired after working tonight—''

"C'mon, Sammy. It'll be the last chance I get to see you before I go on my business trip."

"You're going on a business trip?" Sam's arms tightened around Cassie, causing the little girl to squirm. "For how long?"

"A week or so. Some antitrust issues have cropped up with the sale of RiversWare and I have to go to Washington, D.C., to settle them."

Sam sat in stunned silence at this new disaster. How could she convince him to break off his engagement if he wasn't even here?

Brad adjusted the rearview mirror so he could look at her. "Come to the race, Sammy. It would mean a lot to me if you did."

In spite of her dismay at his news, her heart started to beat in the same irregular rhythm it had in the maze. Brad was too darn used to getting his own way. She'd noticed that about him before. She would probably kill herself if she tried to skate in some dumb race. She had to say no. She couldn't go, no matter how insistent, how intent, how *compelling* the gray-blue eyes in the mirror were....

"Of course I'll come, Brad," she heard herself say.

Chapter Six

Sam arrived at a grungy corner in a run-down area of Hollywood at 11:00 a.m, exactly two hours late. The race appeared to be already over. She saw a group of people with signs apparently protesting something, a couple of skaters—stragglers, maybe—and Brad inspecting cracks in the sidewalk. There was no sign of Heather.

The blonde must have gone home, leaving Brad to wait for Sam. He'd doubtlessly insisted on waiting. Brad was like that. But Heather probably hadn't liked waiting around. The two of them might have even argued about it.

Sam's steps grew a little jauntier. She'd planned on being late. In fact, she'd been so determined to be late, that somehow she'd woken up at 6:00 a.m. Too antsy to go back to sleep, she'd gotten up, dressed in record time and been on the freeway by seven o'clock. She'd had to drive around the city several times and stop for coffee twice to make herself two hours late.

She'd only wanted to miss the race—but now it appeared her tardiness had had an unexpected side benefit. She'd missed Heather, too. She just hoped Brad wasn't mad at her....

He glanced over his shoulder and saw her. He smiled.

Her steps slowed. He really had the nicest smile. It softened his eyes and dispelled the remoteness that sometimes set him a little apart. Her gaze traveled down to his blue-and-white tank top. It clearly revealed that the width of his shoulders was *not* the result of padding. His black running shorts hugged his rear end. Who would have thought that Brad had such well-defined glutes? Or that his thighs and calves were so muscled? Or that the front of the shorts would be so...snug.

"Sam?"

She glanced up, startled, realizing he had turned and was looking at her quizzically.

"I...uh, was just trying to figure what material your shorts are made of," she stammered. "It looks like spandex. Is it?"

"I have no idea," Brad said. "Why don't you look at the tag and see?"

He sounded completely casual, as if looking down his shorts was the most normal thing in the world. And maybe it was. Two years ago, before she'd left for New York and Europe, she would have done it without a second thought. Or would she? That last month, she'd been aware that...oh, good grief, she didn't know what she'd been aware of. She was so confused, she wasn't sure of anything anymore, except that she'd felt strange with him ever since his appearance on the shop's doorstep last Monday, and even more so yesterday in the maze. She felt self-conscious around him.

She didn't like the feeling. She wanted it to go away. She was determined to *make* it go away. And the only way to do that, she decided, was to behave as *un*selfconsciously as possible.

She stepped forward and inserted her fingers between the rear waistband of his shorts, trying not to stare at the small "stork bite" birthmark under her fingers at the small of his back. Turning out the tag, she peered down at the fabric content.

"Nylon," she read out loud. "And spandex. And the pocket is one-hundred-percent polyester—"

"There you two are!" a sultry feminine voice exclaimed. "Samantha, what on earth are you doing?"

Sam released Brad's shorts.

"Hi, Heather," Brad said casually to the blonde as she glided to his side. "Sam was just checking the fabric content of my shorts."

"Oh, was she?"

Sam heard the edge to Heather's voice, even though Brad seemed oblivious. The blonde, immaculate in a hot-pink sports bra and glittery blue short-shorts, looked suspiciously at Samantha. Sam felt as if she'd been caught with her hand in the cookie jar. Which was ridiculous, because she had absolutely *no* interest in Brad's cookies.

"You know how Sam is about material and stuff like that."

"Hmm." The blonde didn't look convinced, but she smiled with sugary sweetness at Sam. "You're late."

"Yes, I know. I overslept. The wedding didn't go well last night. The groom was Cambodian and his mother wasn't happy about him marrying an American girl. I'm so sorry I missed the race."

"What are you talking about?" Heather asked. "The race doesn't start until noon."

"Noon?" Samantha repeated blankly. "But Brad said…" She looked at Brad. He arched his eyebrows. Uneasiness settled in the pit of her stomach, the same as last night, when the groom's smiling mother had stepped forward to offer a traditional Cambodian blessing of pretending to cut the bride's hair. "You said it started at nine." Her voice rose a little shrilly.

Brad shrugged. "You must have misunderstood me."

Two years ago, she would have believed him. "I don't believe you," she said flatly.

A smile tugged at the corner of his mouth. "Well…maybe I did make an allowance for your habitual tardiness."

"Habitual tardiness! Habitual tardiness!" Sam felt a lot like the bride's mother must have when—after seeing her half-bald daughter—she'd gone after the groom's mother with the ceremonial Cambodian sword.

Brad grinned. "Come on, Sam. Everyone knows you're always late."

"I am not!"

"Yes, you are. Just admit it. Admit the truth."

He'd said almost the same thing in the truck on the way to the warehouse. What was with him and the "truth"?

"Really, must you two stand there bickering?" Heather covered a slight yawn with her hand. "Brad,

GET FREE BOOKS and a FREE GIFT WHEN YOU PLAY THE...

Just scratch off the silver box with a coin. Then check below to see the gifts you get!

SLOT MACHINE GAME!

YES! I have scratched off the silver box. Please send me the 2 free Silhouette Romance® books and gift for which I qualify. I understand I am under no obligation to purchase any books, as explained on the back of this card.

315 SDL DRRE   215 SDL DRRU

FIRST NAME   LAST NAME

ADDRESS

APT.#   CITY

STATE/PROV.   ZIP/POSTAL CODE

7	7	7	**Worth TWO FREE BOOKS plus a BONUS Mystery Gift!**
🍒	🍒	🍒	**Worth TWO FREE BOOKS!**
♣	♣	♣	**Worth ONE FREE BOOK!**
🔔	🔔	🍒	**TRY AGAIN!**

Visit us online at www.eHarlequin.com

(S-R-02/03)

DETACH AND MAIL CARD TODAY!

The Silhouette Reader Service™ — Here's how it works:

Accepting your 2 free books and gift places you under no obligation to buy anything. You may keep the books and gift and return the shipping statement marked "cancel." If you do not cancel, about a month later we'll send you 6 additional books and bill you just $3.34 each in the U.S., or $3.80 each in Canada, plus 25¢ shipping & handling per book and applicable taxes if any.* That's the complete price and — compared to cover prices of $3.99 each in the U.S. and $4.50 each in Canada — it's quite a bargain! You may cancel at any time, but if you choose to continue, every month we'll send you 6 more books, which you may either purchase at the discount price or return to us and cancel your subscription.
*Terms and prices subject to change without notice. Sales tax applicable in N.Y. Canadian residents will be charged applicable provincial taxes and GST. Credit or debit balances in a customer's account(s) may be offset by any other outstanding balance owed by or to the customer.

one of the contest organizers wants to talk to you. And Samantha, you need to get your gear on.''

"I...I forgot my skates," Sam improvised madly.

"I brought some for you." Brad handed her a heavy duffel bag. "Knee pads and wrist guards, too."

He and Heather skated off. Left holding the bag, Sam sank down on the curb. Was she actually going to have to skate in this horrible marathon?

Cursing Brad and his obnoxious ploy to get her there on time, she pulled on the brand-new, shiny red-and-black in-line skates, praying that they would be too small or too big. They fit perfectly. Her invective against Brad increasing, she snapped the buckles into place, put on the knee pads and wrist guards and glanced up at the growing number of skaters milling around on the street in front of her. She saw several beach-bunny types in bikini tops, along with their surfer-dude counterparts in board shorts. No Elvises, but there was a group of Frank Sinatra, Dean Martin and Sammy Davis Jr. look-alikes.

Sam took a deep breath and rose to her feet.

Her ankles immediately turned inward.

Her heart sank. How could she possibly do this?

Brad and Heather skated up to her side. "You okay?" he asked. "You look kind of nervous."

"I do?" Sam pushed her hair back from her forehead, trying to act as if skating in marathons was something she did every day. Judging from Brad's suddenly perceptive gaze, however, she didn't think she was succeeding too well. "Well, actually, I am a little nervous about the race. I've never skated so far before."

"It won't be hard," he assured her. "We only have

to go around the course twice—five kilometers in all.''

Five kilometers! Sam calculated quickly in her head. Wasn't that about three miles? Her spirits ebbed to a new low, but she braced herself by reminding herself it was for a good cause. "Let's go," she said bravely. "I want to do my part to help…" She paused, frowning a little. Had Brad or Heather ever said what cause they were supporting? "What charity did you say the race benefits?"

Heather flipped a long strand of hair over her shoulder. "The Society for the Preservation of the Hollywood Tree Rat."

"The Hollywood tree rat?" Sam repeated blankly. She'd never heard of the creature. Nor of any society to save it. Why on earth would anyone want to save rats? She didn't. She was going to have to skate some god-awful number of miles in the hot sun to help save a rodent?

Her shoulders slumped. The next couple of hours were going to be sheer misery.

"It's been a while since I've skated," she said, trying not to sound as wimpy as she felt. "I might not be able to go the whole distance—"

"Don't worry," Brad said. "We'll stay by you and make sure you don't get into trouble."

Heather's lip curled.

Sam's shoulders straightened. Suddenly, she didn't care how long the race was or what it was for. She just wanted Brad to see that expression on Heather's face!

But Brad was looking at his watch and missed Heather's sneer. "Come on, you two. We've got to get to the starting line."

Hope flared inside Sam. She'd spent half the night trying to think of some new plan to break up Brad and Heather to no avail. And now here the answer was right before her eyes. Heather was already showing signs of scorn and impatience. How would the blonde react when she had to hold back for Sam's slower speed? Brad wouldn't like Heather's attitude toward Sam—she knew she could count on the loyalty of his friendship for that, at least. It would give him something to think about while on his business trip, that much was certain.

Buoyed by her thoughts, Sam wobbled her way with Brad and Heather to where the other skaters stood at the starting point. There were probably only about fifty people there, Sam estimated, holding on to Brad's arm to keep from falling down. Apparently not too many people were all that enthusiastic about saving the Hollywood tree rat. In fact, the protesters she'd noticed earlier held signs that read, Death to the Hollywood Tree Rat, and The Only Good Tree Rat Is a Dead One.

Sam felt a secret sympathy for the protesters' sentiments. She loved animals, but rats weren't high on her list. To be perfectly honest, if she had a choice, she would be holding one of those signs herself. She slanted a glance at Brad. Actually, she was surprised he was sponsoring this particular charity. Then again, he was probably supporting Heather more than the event. The Hollywood tree rat sounded like something that the blonde would adore.

A gun went off and the mass of skaters moved forward. Someone bumped against Sam and she would have fallen, but Brad grabbed her around the waist, saving her from an ignominious tumble.

Leaning heavily on Brad, Sam moved her feet back and forth as she skated forward. Within seconds, the rest of the skaters had passed by them and they had a clear path, but Sam barely noticed. Her gaze was fixed firmly on the ground directly in front of her as she expended tremendous amounts of energy to keep going.

Time passed with agonizing slowness. The sun beat down on her; perspiration beaded her brow; her muscles cramped. "How much farther?" she gasped when she could endure it no longer.

"Only about 4.99 kilometers," Brad said encouragingly.

Heather snorted in disgust. "At this rate, it will take us two years to complete the course."

In spite of her agony, Sam was delighted to see Brad frown at Heather. "She's trying," he said sternly.

Heather immediately looked contrite. "I'm sorry, I didn't mean to sound impatient. It's only that we'll raise more money for the Hollywood tree rat if we complete the course."

"That's true." Brad nodded thoughtfully. "Perhaps you should go on ahead."

"Oh, I can't do that! I would feel terrible leaving you and Samantha to inch your way around the course."

"Don't worry, we'll manage," Brad said, his gaze meeting Heather's.

Heather's lashes dropped. "If you're sure…"

"I'm sure." There was an ironic tone in Brad's voice that Sam didn't quite understand.

"Well, if you insist." With a little wave, Heather glided off with long, powerful strokes of her legs.

Sam watched the blonde go, her heart sinking. There was no chance of Heather's revealing her true nature if she wasn't even around. So much for her plan.

"You're doing great, Sam."

Samantha glanced up at Brad, smiling automatically. His gray-blue eyes smiled back at her, his arm around her waist strong and firm, his fingers resting lightly on her hip....

Her skate slid in a weird direction. Losing her balance, she felt herself going down. Her arms flailed. A scream rose in her throat.

Suddenly, a steely arm clamped around her waist, pressing her against rock-solid muscle.

"Are you okay?" Brad asked, supporting her weight easily.

She regained her balance, but her heartbeat didn't resume its normal pace. Her shirt had pulled up and his arm and hand squeezed against her skin. Rough hair on his leg scratched against her thigh. The heat of the day seemed to extend down inside her, starting from the areas where his skin pressed against hers.

"Sammy?"

"I think I need to rest for a few minutes," she said. Eight years ago the same thing had happened at the roller rink and Sam had burst into laughter. But she didn't feel like laughing this time.

He directed her to the curb, got her a bottle of water and sat down next to her. She pressed the ice-cold bottle against her wrists and her neck and her waist and her thigh while she watched three skaters who had completed the first lap of the race zoom by.

"I don't see Heather yet," Brad commented.

The name was more effective than the icy water

bottle at cooling Sam's heated skin. She took a deep breath.

"Brad…"

"Yes?"

"I hope Heather won't be annoyed with me for slowing the two of you down."

"Don't worry. Heather's not like that."

"Maybe you need to get your contacts checked," Sam muttered.

"What?" Brad bent his ear toward her. "I didn't hear you."

"I said she seemed a little ticked when she left us."

"She's just very concerned about helping the Hollywood tree rat."

"Oh, yes." Sam fiddled with her elbow pad. "Um…do *you* care anything about the Hollywood tree rat?"

"Whatever Heather cares about, I care about."

Sam drew in a breath, her lungs suddenly starting to hurt even though she'd stopped skating. He really loved Heather a lot. He was going to be terribly hurt when he discovered what a hateful, treacherous woman she was. He didn't deserve that. He really didn't. She wished there was some way she could spare him that pain.

"Ready to rejoin the race?" he asked.

"No," she said, unable to look at him. "I must have twisted my ankle or something."

"We'd better check to make sure it's not sprained." Before she could stop him, he crouched in front of her and unbuckled her skate.

"Oh, no, you don't have to do that!" she protested. "I'm sure it's nothing serious."

"You can't be too careful," he said cheerfully as he tugged her skate off.

It felt wonderful to have the cumbersome thing off. A small sigh of relief escaped her.

Brad glanced up. "Did I hurt you?"

"Um...a little," she lied.

He stripped off her sock, too, then put his hands on her ankle and pressed lightly. "Does that hurt?" he asked.

Gooseflesh tingled up her leg, but it didn't really hurt. "Do you even know what you're looking for?"

"No, not really."

Her gaze flew to his, her lips parting. She stared at him, seeing the slight smile curving his mouth, the sun glinting off his hair and the matching glint in eyes that looked a very bright blue. She tried to pull her foot away, but his hold tightened. His smile faded, his thumb absently stroked her ankle. His eyes grew more serious, more intent. Her mouth suddenly felt dry. Those eyes seemed to be coming closer. And closer...

"Good heavens!" a female voice exclaimed. "What are you two doing, sitting here on the curb?"

"Just resting my ankle," Sam said brightly as Heather stopped in front of them. Perhaps a shade *too* brightly. She closed her eyes and pretended to be resting.

She heard the clink of Brad's skates as he stood up and moved away. She heard a murmur of voices. Opening her eyes, she saw Brad talking to Heather. He did not look pleased.

"I'm sorry," Sam heard Heather say. "I didn't realize—" The blonde's gaze met Sam's for a moment, then moved back to Brad. "I'll make it up to you later, darling,'' Heather cooed, slipping her arms around Brad's neck. ''I promise.''

Sam averted her gaze quickly. She felt sick to her stomach. The heat must have affected her more than she'd realized.

''I'll go get the car,'' Brad said, still looking a little grim.

As soon as he was a safe distance away, Heather gave Sam a vicious look. ''I get it now—you want him for yourself. I can't believe I didn't see that immediately. Well, you'd better forget it, bitch. Brad would never be interested in a plain little nobody like you. I doubt he's even aware you're a woman. So if you're thinking of trying to seduce Brad, forget it. He would laugh in your face.''

Chapter Seven

Heather skated away. Sam stared after her, her fingernails digging into the concrete sidewalk. The *nerve* of the woman. The unbelievable *gall*. It would serve her right if Sam *did* seduce Brad. That would be one surefire way to break up the engagement. She could invite Brad to her apartment and lure him into her bedroom. She could stand up on tiptoe, wrap her arms around his neck and press her mouth against his....

Her breath caught. What was she thinking? Brad was her friend. She couldn't do that to him. Besides, she was no seductress. Even if she tried to seduce him, she doubted he would succumb.

Or would he?

She remembered the way he'd been looking at her just a few minutes ago. It was the same way he'd looked at her when they were in the maze. For a few brief moments, she could have almost sworn that he was going to kiss her....

No. Sam bent over her skate, tugging at the stiff

buckles. He was an engaged man. He had no business kissing anyone other than his fiancée. Not that Sam wanted him to kiss Heather, but still, it didn't speak well of his character to want to kiss someone else. In fact, it seemed completely *out* of character.

Maybe it had just been an odd impulse. Or maybe he'd been curious and wanted to take the opportunity before he became a married man. Maybe he wondered what it would be like to kiss her. She wondered herself…oh, for heaven's sake.

She yanked off her skate. She must have been mistaken. She'd never been able to tell what he was thinking. He'd probably just been going to plant a kiss on her cheek or her forehead or the tip of her nose. He would never *really* try to kiss her. If he did, everything would get complicated. It could ruin their friendship.

And their friendship meant way too much to her to ever let that happen.

Sam had a hard time sleeping that night. Her tiny, unair-conditioned apartment was hot and stuffy, and she felt restless. She tried to go to sleep, but every time she dozed off she dreamed of a seagull with gray-blue eyes kissing a brunette seagull that croaked breathlessly, "We're just friends."

Every muscle aching, wearing caked concealer under her eyes to hide the dark rings, Sam limped into the bridal shop Monday morning to find Jeanette busily inputting something into the computer and Kristin kneeling by several large cartons. The two of them took one look at her, then exchanged meaningful glances.

"What?" Sam asked defensively.

"I told you it was a stupid idea for you to try to go to an in-line skating race." Kristin, wearing denim capris and a white tube top, ripped the masking tape off a carton. The sound grated on Sam's already tender nerves. "You look like someone dug you up out of a graveyard."

Jeanette, wearing a gray suit that made her look like a prison guard, pushed her chunky black glasses up on her forehead. "What happened? Are you all right? Did you hurt yourself?" she demanded, sounding—and looking—a lot like their mother.

"I'm fine." Sam glanced at the mannequin on the dais. Miss Blogden's gown was gone. In its place was a skimpy white dress that looked a lot like the teddy Sam wore to bed. "Just a bit sore."

"Did you make a total fool of yourself in front of Heather?" Kristin asked with her usual sisterly tact.

Sam glared at her, then sighed. "Pretty much. She did get nasty when she saw how slow I was, and I hoped Brad would notice, but he didn't." She hobbled over to the sofa and lowered herself carefully. "It seems hopeless. Brad's going to be gone a whole week and I don't know what else I can do."

"It's just as well." Jeanette returned her attention to the spreadsheet on the computer and started typing again. "I thought you were crazy to interfere from the beginning."

Sam's brows drew together. She was getting tired of the lack of support from her sisters. Where was their family loyalty? They just didn't seem to understand how important it was to save Brad.

"Anyway," Jeanette continued, "there's no way anyone could get Heather to seem anything other than a nice woman."

"Except for Mom," Kristin said absently as she lifted a plastic-wrapped gown from the carton. "She can get anyone's goat."

"Kristin!" Jeanette said in reproof.

Sam straightened a little. "What did you say, Kristin?"

Kristin hung the dress on a rail and pulled off the plastic. "I said, Mom could get anyone's goat." She glanced over her shoulder. "You know it's true, Jeanette."

"Brad and Heather and dinner at Mom's," Sam said thoughtfully. "It might work."

Jeanette's frown moved from Kristin to Sam. "Now, Samantha…"

"Hey, you're right." Kristin wadded the plastic into a ball. "If Mom's inquisition techniques don't drive Heather insane, then listening to Dave will."

"Kristin!" Jeanette's protest sounded a little half-hearted. "You shouldn't talk about Mother's husband that way."

"Why not? Even you said he was as bland as a boiled potato when Mom married him." Kristin frowned. "Or did you say he *looked* like a boiled potato—?"

"Never mind," Jeanette said hastily. "I admit he's a bit…dull, but that's no reason to be disrespectful."

Kristin grumbled, but Sam paid little attention. An image rose in her mind of Brad and Heather at dinner with Vera and Dave. Her plump, tiny mother might look like a friendly chipmunk, but she had the instincts of a rabid wolverine when she disliked someone. Heather wouldn't have a chance.

"I think it might work." Sam stared at the headless mannequin, her brow furrowed in thought. "I can ask

Mom to invite them to dinner as soon as Brad gets back from his trip. Mom will disapprove of Heather because she's an actress and Heather will hate Mom and Dave. Heather won't like it at all when she finds out that Brad expects to spend holidays with them.''

"Humph." Jeanette didn't stop typing. "It sounds pretty far-fetched to me. And Mom won't like your plan at all."

"I won't tell her. She'd probably ruin everything if I did. You know how she is. Remember when you brought Matt home and she looked him up and down and said, 'So you're the boy that—'"

"Yes, I remember," Jeanette interrupted quickly, with a meaningful glance toward Kristin.

"Oh, I know Matt knocked you up and that you had to get married in a rush." Kristin tossed the plastic toward the wastebasket—the crinkly ball went right in. "I can count, you know."

Sam took one look at Jeanette's face and coughed. "Yes, well, just think what Mom might say to Heather. Probably something like, 'So Samantha tells me that you're only marrying Brad for his money.' She could ruin the whole plan."

"I don't know," Jeanette said stiffly, still glaring at Kristin. "I have a bad feeling about this."

"What are you, a psychic?" Sam was getting a little tired of Jeanette's negative attitude. "It's worth a try, at least. It's not like anything terrible can happen. Right?"

Jeanette didn't look convinced, and in spite of herself, Sam felt a twinge of doubt. So far, her record on outwitting Heather was pretty dismal. There wouldn't be much time before the wedding to try something else if this scheme failed...

It wouldn't, she told herself as she picked up the phone and dialed. But maybe she should have a backup plan, just to be on the safe side—

"Hi, Mom? Could you do me a favor? Could you invite Brad and Heather to dinner next week? Yeah, I thought you'd want to meet her before the wedding. Yeah. Oh, didn't Kristin tell you? She's an actress...."

Chapter Eight

Vera Gillespie had met Dave Evans at a Garden Club meeting right after she divorced Sam's father. The two had married a few years later and moved into Dave's muddy-green tract home. Built in the seventies, it had its original green appliances and matching green carpet. Sam had always felt pretty much the same about the house as she did about Dave. Or at least she had until tonight.

"I'm having a lot of trouble with my Zutano avocado tree." Speaking with a slightly nasal twang, Dave rested his elbows on the green Formica table as he leaned toward Heather. "Anthracnose fungus kept attacking it. I sprayed the Zutano with dodine, which helped, but then I noticed some brownish patches on the leaves. I recognized it immediately—the Cercospera fungus. Nasty stuff, Cercospera. Neutral copper's the only way to kill it. But the scab fungus is even worse. I nearly lost my whole crop...."

Dave, his bald pate shining faintly green—either a

reflection from the room's chartreuse walls or maybe from eating too many avocados—wore a leafy Hawaiian shirt and olive twill shorts. He had barely touched the chicken enchilada on his plate. He was too busy educating Heather on the various kinds of avocado fungi.

Heather, a frozen smile pasted on her face, appeared stunned.

Sam had been shocked when her mother married Dave. She couldn't understand how Vera could be attracted to someone so ordinary—especially after being married to a man as dynamic as Jack Gillespie.

But tonight, for the first time, Sam felt a certain appreciation for Dave. In fact, as she watched Heather's eyes glaze over, Sam wanted to hug him.

Her mother, too. Vera, a beige-polyester-slacks older version of Jeanette, hadn't been at all taken in by Heather's daisy-sprigged cotton dress and prim little straw purse laced with blue ribbon. During the first part of the meal, her questions had gradually grown more and more personal. Her round, chipmunk face had somehow taken on the harsh angles of a predator as her unmistakable disapproval of Heather increased.

In Sam's opinion, the evening was progressing beautifully. For the first time since Brad had left on his business trip a week and a half ago, Sam didn't feel sick to her stomach. The night wasn't even half over, and already Heather looked as though she couldn't wait to escape. Sam was sure the only thing that had kept her from running screaming from the house was Brad.

Brad…Sam glanced across the table at him. His khakis and button-down shirt were as casual and relaxed as he appeared to be—but so far he'd managed to protect Heather by inserting a question or a joke whenever the blonde looked as if she was going to retort to one of Vera's more offensive remarks.

He maneuvered the conversation so subtly and so skillfully that Sam probably wouldn't have been aware of it except that she was trying to seize control herself. Incredibly, she couldn't grab it away from Brad. She'd been tempted several times to leap across the table and gag him with her napkin.

She comforted herself with the thought that he hadn't really been too successful at diversion. He'd changed the subject to avocados when Vera's questions got too intense—but judging from Heather's glazed eyes, his efforts had backfired. Besides, Sam knew that her mother couldn't be put off for long.

Sure enough, when Dave started talking about red spider mites and red-banded thrips, Vera wrested the conversation away from her husband and continued her effort to ''get to know''—as she considered her ruthless interrogation—Brad's fiancée.

''So, you're getting married in three days.'' Vera's gaze raked over Heather. ''What's the big rush? Are you pregnant?''

''Just in love,'' Brad answered with a fond smile at the blonde.

Vera didn't appear much impressed by Brad's silliness. ''I've heard stories about actresses,'' she informed Heather. ''Don't you have to sleep with someone to get a part?''

Sam, sitting across the table from Heather, saw the blonde's grip on her fork tighten just a fraction. Sam set down her glass of iced tea and waited.

''Those kinds of things don't happen very much anymore, Vera,'' Brad interrupted smoothly. ''Everyone is too worried about being accused of sexual harassment. You have to rely on hard work and talent nowadays.''

"Humph.'' The news that the film industry wasn't one huge solid mass of sordid sexual shenanigans appeared to disappoint Vera. "But you still have to be willing to take off all your clothes in front of the camera to get a part, right?''

Brad choked a little on a mouthful of spicy beans. "Most actresses have very high moral standards—and are very active in various charities. In fact, Heather was instrumental in arranging the recent in-line skating race Sam skated in.''

"Samantha didn't tell me about any race.'' Vera glanced at her daughter, then aimed her suspicious gaze at Heather. "A race, eh? What charity was this for?''

"The Society for the Preservation of the Hollywood Tree Rat,'' Heather said.

Vera's jaw dropped. "You raised money to save rats?''

"It's a very rare species.'' Heather smiled sweetly.

Vera spooned some corn onto her plate. "I wouldn't have thought so.''

Heather inhaled. A glitter appeared in her large blue eyes.

"I just had the exterminator out to get rid of the rats in our yard.'' Oblivious to the tension, Dave took a second helping of guacamole. "They were eating my avocados.''

"I hope the exterminator checked to make sure they weren't Hollywood tree rats,'' Heather said.

"How can you tell a Hollywood tree rat from a regular one?'' Dave asked.

"The Hollywood tree rat is blond and very sleek and elegant." Heather took a dainty bite of her salad. "It is vastly superior to the average, run-of-the-mill tree rat."

Vera's nose twitched. She shifted her bulk in her chair. "Sounds like a perfectly useless rodent, if you ask me. And I'll bet they sleep around, too."

Heather's knuckles turned white on her knife. Very carefully she laid down the utensil and looked directly at Vera. Vera, her nostrils flaring, put down the serving spoon and met the blonde's gaze head-on.

Sam could almost see the red flag waving and the two women pawing their hooves. She took a tortilla chip, pushed the basket aside and leaned forward. Heather's mouth opened.

"Vera," Brad said calmly, "did I tell you that Sam, Heather and I took Jeanette's kids to the maze before I went on my trip? The kids had a great time."

Vera tore her gaze from Heather's. "Yes, Jeanette mentioned it," the older woman said.

"Heather and I had a great time, also," Brad continued. "Especially Heather. She was really impressed by Audrey, Brendan and Cassie."

Sam saw the slight start the blonde gave, but when Vera looked over, Heather's expression was perfectly in control.

"They are wonderful children, Mrs. Evans," Heather said.

"Heather commented on the fact that they are extraordinarily attractive," Brad added.

To Sam's dismay, Vera's expression softened perceptibly. "They *are* beautiful, aren't they?"

"Yes, indeed." Brad spooned some more salsa onto his enchilada. "But they have more than just good looks. There's something about them that you don't often see, something 'unique,' as Heather put it.''

Vera's chest swelled to the proportions of a piñata. ''*I've* always thought they were special. Jeanette and I have talked about it many times.''

''Heather wondered if Jeanette has ever thought of having them try out to become child models?'' Brad speared a bit of enchilada with his fork. ''It can be quite lucrative.''

''Oh, no, they should have a normal childhood.'' But Vera looked pleased, nonetheless.

''Hmm, very wise of you. But perhaps you would do Heather and me a favor. Heather was so impressed by the children, she asked Jeanette if Audrey could act as a junior bridesmaid and Brendan as ring bearer. Cassie is already going to be flower girl, of course. But Jeanette said no, that she thought the three of them together might cause trouble—''

''My grandchildren never cause trouble!'' Vera exclaimed, apparently forgetting the three broken windows, the decapitated stone dwarf in the garden and Dave's dentures, which were found half buried in the back yard.

''Could you talk to Jeanette?'' Brad asked. ''Convince her to let the children be in the wedding?''

''Of course I will.'' Vera was flushed and glowing. ''Jeanette worries way too much....''

Sam leaned back in her chair, her anticipation crumbling like her chip as she bit into it. Heather had been about to explode, she was sure. If only Brad hadn't interfered.

She glanced at him, only to find him watching her, a smile playing around the corners of his mouth.

When he saw her looking at him, the smile immediately disappeared and his expression grew bland. He took a bite of enchilada and turned his attention back to Vera, who was telling Heather about Audrey's prize-winning essay, Brendan's winning basket in the recent championship game and Cassie's starring role in the dance recital.

Why was he looking so smug? Sam wondered crossly. He had that look on his face that she couldn't stand—the one that seemed to say, "I know exactly what you're thinking."

What she hated even more was, he almost always *did* know. But he couldn't this time. If he suspected she was trying to break up his engagement, he would be furious. He still thought Heather was perfect—his phone calls from Washington D.C. more than proved that.

"Heather never complains," he'd explained the first night he called. "So I'm relying on you, Sammy, to tell me if anything's wrong with her."

There was a *lot* wrong—so she'd tried to tell him. Unfortunately, even the slightest criticism of Heather caused Brad to launch into a hyperbolic paean of praise to the blonde. Boredom—and a weak stomach—had frequently forced Sam to change the subject. When she did, the conversation always flowed more easily. In fact, on several occasions, they'd ended up talking for hours.

If it hadn't been for the days passing by and the date of his wedding looming closer and closer, she might have enjoyed the conversations. Brad was much easier to talk to on the phone. She didn't feel all unsettled, the way she did when she was with him. Sometimes, after she'd hung up, she'd lain in bed, staring through the dark, wishing it could always be like that with him. She wished it could be the way it had been when they were in high school together....

She added some sugar to her tea, watching Brad as she stirred. Things would never be the same if she didn't get rid of Heather. She'd dropped a few hints about the blonde this last week, but Brad had brushed off her comments. He wouldn't give up on Heather easily—not unless he saw evidence of her true nature with his own eyes.

"Are you sure you don't want any enchiladas, Heather?" Sam asked with false solicitousness.

"No, thank you," Heather replied.

As Sam had hoped, Vera turned her gaze to the blonde's plate.

"Is that all you're going to eat, Heather?"

To Sam's disappointment, her mother's tone was much milder than before. But her hopes rose when Vera continued, "Is something wrong with you? You're not anorexic, are you?"

"No, Mrs. Evans," Heather replied. "The food looks delicious, but I'm appearing in a commercial and the director told me I had to lose five pounds."

"I don't approve of young women eating so little." Vera's face took on that Feed-the-Children maternal look—not at all the reaction Sam had been hoping for. "It's not healthy. Didn't your mother teach you about the effects of malnutrition?"

Brad put his arm around Heather's shoulders. "Her mother didn't have much of a chance to teach her anything," he said in a low voice. "Her mother died when Heather was twelve."

Silence fell around the table. Even Vera was quiet for a few seconds.

"I'm so sorry, my dear," Vera finally said. "Growing up without your mother must have been very hard on you—and on your father."

"Her father died at the same time," Brad said. "Heather was devastated. Isn't that right, sweetheart?"

Heather, her gaze lowered, nodded almost imperceptibly.

"How did they die?" Vera asked.

"In an accident." Brad glanced at Heather, whose lips were trembling with distress, then continued. "They were driving home from a trip to the East Coast—where they'd gone to donate bone marrow for cancer research—when their car was attacked by a bull with mad cow disease. Heather's parents got out of the car to try to calm the poor beast and they were gored."

Sam frowned. "Mad cow disease? I thought that was only a problem in Europe—"

"Samantha!" her mother exclaimed. "Are you accusing Heather of making up this terrible story?"

"I was just asking a question...." Everyone at the table was staring at her as though *she* had mad cow disease. "I'm sorry, Heather," she mumbled. "I didn't mean to imply anything."

Dave and Vera had already turned their attention back to Heather. Dave had tears in his eyes.

"Would you like some guacamole?" he asked Heather, offering the bowl.

Heather took a small dollop and placed it on her salad.

"You poor, dear child!" Vera also had tears in her eyes. "What happened to you?"

"Her grandparents took her in," Brad said.

Vera reached over and clasped the blonde's hand. "Thank heaven you had someone."

"Yes, I was very grateful," Heather murmured.

"They did their best for her," Brad said. "Even though they were invalids."

"Invalids! But...who took care of them?"

"Heather did."

"It was the least I could do." Heather spoke with a slight quaver in her voice. "And I really didn't mind. I would have had to go to the orphanage if it weren't for them. Although sometimes it was difficult to care for them and go to school and work nights—"

"You had to work? But you were just a child!"

"Money was extremely tight." Heather's voice grew stronger. "Fortunately, I looked older, so I was able to get a job at the local Big Boy's. I didn't care that I had to wear clothes from the thrift store or eat macaroni and cheese for dinner every night as long as my grandparents and I were together."

Dave took a deep breath. "I'll give you some avocados to take home."

"You are the bravest girl I ever heard of." Vera dabbed at her eyes. "Brad, you make sure you take care of this child. She deserves it after all she's been through."

Heather deserved an Oscar, not avocados, Sam thought. Dave and Vera had fallen for the blonde's tale like a couple who'd seen an image of the Virgin Mary in the stain on their bathtub. Sam was willing to bet her favorite Ralph Lauren cowhide purse that Heather had made the whole thing up. But she knew no one would believe her—unless she had proof.

"I plan to treat her like a princess, don't worry," Brad said, gazing adoringly at Heather.

Sam bit down hard on a tortilla chip. How could a successful businessman be so gullible? She'd always thought him pretty sharp when it came to people. He'd summed up several of her ex-boyfriends—Pete as a controlling bully, Terry as a dependent wimp and Stewart as a self-centered bore—within two minutes of meeting them. So how could he be so blind about Heather?

Sam stabbed at her salsa with her chip, only half listening as her mother wiped her eyes and blew her nose.

"You know," Vera said, "maybe being an actress isn't really that bad. But fortunately, you won't have to keep working once you get married. Marriage and children are the most wonderful things in the world—although *some* people don't seem to think so."

Sam stopped poking the salsa and glanced warily at her mother. Sure enough, Vera's laserlike gaze was fixed upon her daughter.

Sam groaned inwardly.

"If only *Samantha* would settle down and get married," Vera continued, her voice growing a little shrill as she spoke the oft-repeated words. "She seems perfectly content to lead an aimless life—"

"Mom…"

"And the way she goes through boyfriends—"

"Mom…"

"What was that last one's name? The one you brought to Christmas dinner when you returned from Europe. Jean-Paul? What happened to him?"

He'd been pushing her to get married, that's what'd happened to him. Sam suspected he'd been more interested in getting his residency status than in her, but she didn't tell her mother that. "Mom, I've told you before, I want to establish my career before I get married."

"Career! What career? Three years of community college and you still couldn't decide. If you'd only stuck with it, you'd have your accounting degree by now."

Sam's head began to ache. She loved her mother dearly, but she hated it when Vera got in one of her nagging moods. She was trying to figure out what to do with her life, she really was. The answer just kept eluding her....

"It's obvious what Sam is destined to do." Brad spoke quietly, but his deep voice carried clearly around the table. "She's going to become a fashion designer."

Everyone turned and stared at him—including Sam, her mouth falling open.

"A fashion designer? But Samantha has terrible taste in clothes." Vera frowned at a spot of salsa on her yellow-and-purple floral blouse. She wiped it off with her napkin.

"She was a little avant-garde when she was younger," Brad said. "But she definitely has talent. There's no reason she can't go back to college. I have a friend who works at a design institute. I'll call him tomorrow, Sammy, if you want me to."

"Humph," Vera said before Sam could reply. "I still think marriage would be better. Every woman needs a man—"

"It's important to find the right one, though," Brad said. "I waited a long time to find Heather, but it was worth it. It's better to wait for the love of your life than settle for second best. Wouldn't you agree, Vera?"

Vera glanced at Dave, who was scooping up avocado dip with a chip. A tender light lit her eyes. "Yes," she said softly. "Look what happened to me. I had one disastrous marriage because I couldn't wait—"

"Mom," Sam interrupted. "Didn't I smell strawberry pie when we arrived? I'll go get it."

Inside the kitchen, she leaned against the refrigerator and closed her eyes. She'd wanted to get away from the dining room, partly to avoid hearing her mother complain about Dad, but even more, so she could think about what Brad had said. A fashion designer—of course! That was exactly what she wanted to do. Why hadn't she realized it before? It seemed so obvious. But she hadn't even thought of it until Brad said the words.

Brad...how had he known? Sometimes she thought he knew her better than she knew herself. She'd missed him the last couple of years, more than she'd realized. When she'd been in New York and Europe, she'd been terribly homesick—for her family, she'd thought. But everything inside her hadn't lit up when she saw her mother and sisters the way it had when she'd seen him. He was a true friend. No, more than a friend. He was... He was...

The kitchen door swung open, and Sam straightened when she saw Heather entering the kitchen.

The elation inside Sam quickly dwindled. She'd almost forgotten about Heather. Heather, who was going to make Brad miserable if Sam didn't stop her.

The blonde glanced around the green kitchen. "I offered to come get the dessert plates and forks—it seemed the only way to get away from that old battle-ax."

Sam opened her mouth to make a sharp retort, then checked herself. This was it—the opportunity she'd been waiting for.

She slipped her hand into her pocket.

"I'm sorry about your parents," she said to the blonde. "Being gored by a bull with mad cow disease must be a horrible way to die."

Heather let out a crack of laughter. "That was a pretty sappy story, wasn't it?"

"Sappy?" Sam asked, pretending innocence.

"You didn't really believe it, did you? All that crap about my invalid grandparents and being glad I didn't have to go to the orphanage? Man, are you stupid. I told Brad that tale to make him feel sorry for me." Heather smiled. "It worked, too."

Sam had to stifle an urge to slap the smile off the blonde's face. "Do you care even the least little bit for Brad?" she asked. "Do you feel anything at all?"

"Please, don't get all indignant and self-righteous on me. You obviously have your own stake in all this. You've made it pretty clear you want his money for yourself."

"That's not true! I don't care anything about his money!"

"Yeah, right. You expect me to believe you're doing all of this because you *love* him."

"I do love him. But not the way you mean. We're friends, and I want him to be happy."

"You expect me to believe that your interest in a rich, sexy, good-looking guy like Brad is purely platonic? Give me a break."

Sam glared at her. "You obviously know nothing about friendship."

"Uh-huh. And you obviously know nothing about sex—"

Beep! Beep! Beep!

Heather stopped abruptly, staring at Sam's pocket. "What's that?"

In the heat of the argument, Sam had forgotten her backup plan. She pulled out the tiny electronic gadget she'd purchased that morning and showed it to the blonde. "Just a tape recorder."

"A tape recorder?"

For once the blonde sounded disconcerted. Sam reveled in the moment. She rewound the tape. "I think Brad is going to be very interested to hear *this*." Triumphantly, she pressed the play button.

There was a few seconds of static. Then a click. And then...the sound of two muffled, indistinguishable voices.

Sam stared at the recorder in horror.

Heather burst into laughter. "Wow, Brad's really going to be interested in hearing that. Didn't you even test that piece of junk? Not that it would have mattered." Heather picked up the plates and headed for the door. "It's pretty obvious that you're lacking even the most basic equipment to hold the interest of a man like Brad."

The blonde's laughter echoing in her ears, Sam clenched her teeth, her fists and even her toes. She'd thought she'd hated Blanche Milken and even Dave when he married her mother. She realized now she'd never known what true hate was.

Until she met Heather Lovelace.

Her lips pressed in a tight line, she picked up the pie and marched out to the dining room.

The rest of the evening passed in a blur. Only one thought was uppermost in her mind.

She would do anything to stop the blonde.

Anything.

Chapter Nine

"**Y**ou're going to do *what*?"

Sam winced a little and held the phone away from her ear at Kristin's incredulous shout. The plan she'd formed while watching her mother and Dave fuss and coo over Heather had seemed brilliant last night but was sounding a bit wild in the light of day. After the humiliating failure of her tape-recording scheme, however, she really had no choice.

Sam glanced out of the door of the wedding shop's small office to where Jeanette was talking to a short, plaid woman with a tall, polka-dot daughter. Quietly, not wanting to disturb Jeanette—and not wanting her negative older sister to overhear—Sam closed the door and repeated into the phone, "I'm going to get Brad in a compromising position. When Heather sees us together, she'll have to break off the engagement."

"That's what I thought you said." Kristin was silent for a moment. "I think you need a vacation. A nice long vacation."

"For heaven's sake, Kristin!" Sam clutched the phone more tightly. "Just a few years ago, you loved nothing better than to pop up unexpectedly whenever I brought a date home. I'd think you'd love the chance to do it again."

"I've grown up since then," Kristin said loftily.

With an effort, Sam restrained her exasperation. "Please, Kristin. The wedding is the day after tomorrow. We have to stop him from marrying Heather."

"I don't see why. She seems like a nice-enough woman."

"Kristin! I told you what she said to me in the kitchen at Mom's house. Not to mention what she said before in the rest room at the restaurant. She's evil. Pure evil."

"Oh, yeah. Right. Well, you are my sister, and I suppose I believe you."

"Thanks," Sam said, rather dryly. Kristin's statement wasn't exactly a declaration of unquestioning sisterly faith, but she supposed it would have to suffice. "Now, do you understand what I want you to do?"

"It's not that hard to understand. You want me to bring Heather to the shop at ten-thirty this evening. Although how I'm supposed to accomplish that, I don't know. Couldn't we come earlier?"

"Mrs. Kennedy has an appointment at six-thirty and you know how long *she* usually takes. There's no way I'll be able to get rid of her until nine or nine-thirty. Tell Heather it's to check the menu or something."

"To check the menu! At ten-thirty at night? She'd have to be an idiot to believe that!"

Sam sighed impatiently. Kristin was being uncommonly thick today. "I don't care what you tell her—just tell her something. Okay?"

"Okay," Kristin said obediently, if a bit doubtfully.

"Thank you," Sam said, and hung up the phone. Really, Kristin had never quite outgrown her childhood habit of being amazingly annoying at times.

Picking up the phone again, she dialed Brad's number. He answered after two rings.

"Hello?"

The muscles in her stomach contracted unexpectedly at the sound of his voice.

You expect me to believe that your interest in a rich, sexy, good-looking guy like Brad is purely platonic?

Sam brushed away the memory of Heather's cynical words and took a deep breath. "Hello, Brad? This is Samantha. I need to talk to you, and I was wondering if you could stop by the shop tonight at ten."

He was silent for a moment. "Tonight at ten?"

Sam twisted the cord around her finger. "Yes. I, um, have to go out today and that's the only time I can see you." She felt remarkably foolish as she made the weak explanation. Maybe Kristin had been right, after all.

"All right, I'll be there," he said after another slight pause.

She felt even more foolish that night, after Mrs. Kennedy left, waiting for his arrival. She paced around the shop, nervously assessing the preparations she'd made. The Celine Dion CD playing softly in the background—was it too sticky sweet? The perfume she was wearing—was the honeysuckle scent too heavily applied? The clinging, low-necked slip dress she wore—was it too blatantly revealing?

She stopped in front of the triple mirror and assessed her appearance. The pale peach fabric clung to her like a second skin, nearly invisible. Her reflection showed masses of dark, curly hair, wide green-gold eyes and pale, freckled skin. Would Brad find her attractive? She didn't know. What if she couldn't get him to kiss her? Maybe she should have chosen a more intimate setting—like her apartment. But it would have been harder to get Heather to come to her apartment.

A knock sounded at the shop door at nine-thirty. Frowning, she went to the door and opened it. Brad stood lounging against the jamb. Dressed casually in blue jeans and a T-shirt, he looked tall and muscled and…*male*. Her breath stuck in her throat.

His gaze swept over her, his eyes widening a little as he took in her outfit. When he glanced up again, he gave her a penetrating stare; then he smiled lazily.

"Hi, Sammy. You look amazingly gorgeous."

"You're early." She gulped in air, trying to steady her nerves.

His brows rose. "Only a minute or two."

She looked at her watch again, and noticed the second hand wasn't moving. "Oh, bother!" she exclaimed, holding it up to her ear. No *tick, tick, tick.* "The battery must be dead. I'll have to get a new one."

"Are you going to let me in?"

"Um, yes, of course." Awkwardly, she stepped back from the door, feeling a strange sense of déjà vu.

He entered the shop. Uneasily, Sam wondered how

much time she had before Kristin and Heather arrived. She wished there was a clock in the showroom. When Jeanette had first opened the shop, she hadn't wanted the customers to feel rushed. What a stupid idea, Sam thought. Jeanette should have gotten a clock.

Taking another gulp of air, she crossed over to the worktable and unrolled a bolt of sapphire-blue satin. She wasn't exactly sure how to proceed. She felt remarkably stupid. How on earth did one go about seducing an engaged man?

"What did you want to talk to me about?"

His voice, so close behind her, made her jump. She licked her lips. What would he do if she threw her arms around his neck and kissed him? Would he kiss her back? Or would he push her away and look at her with disgust?

Her stomach churned. She didn't think she could go through with this. "I…um…wondered if everything is okay with you and Heather." Nervously, she smoothed the rippled satin out with her fingers.

"Everything's fine. Why do you ask?"

Sam risked a quick peek at him. He was standing even closer than she'd thought, so close that if she turned, her shoulder would almost brush against his chest. She could smell denim and cotton and the faint, nearly imperceptible scent of masculine sweat. Brad and sweat? The two didn't go together. She always thought of him sitting at a computer terminal, perfectly calm and cool and sweat-free.

It must be the heat. It was terribly warm in here. "Have you noticed something a little bit odd about Heather?" she asked.

"Like what?" Brad's breath was warm against her cheek.

Sam could hardly breathe at all. "Well…that rat marathon, for one. Aren't you a little surprised that she didn't choose a more…worthwhile charity to support?"

"But that's one of the things I love about Heather—she's so kind and generous, she will help even the most unattractive, unlovable creatures. And she's not afraid to embrace a cause that some might find strange. It takes a lot of courage to do that."

"Hmm. That may be true," Sam murmured. Inwardly, she cursed Brad's habit of always looking for the best in people. "But what about your wedding? She said she doesn't have many friends, but she's invited hundreds of people."

"That's not so strange. She has a lot of business acquaintances. No one she can really confide in, though. That's why she's been trying so hard to make friends with you."

Yeah, right.

"I'm concerned about you." She smoothed a non-existent wrinkle from the blue satin. "And Heather. I think…I'm afraid she may not feel the same way about you as you do about her."

From the corner of her eye, she saw him smile. "Oh, but she does. I'm certain about that."

"Brad…" She turned toward him, groping for words as she stared at the angle of his jaw, the shadow of a faint beard on his chin. That damnable chin. "Women…women are not always honest about their feelings."

"Oh?"

"Some women might marry a man because he was wealthy."

"Would you ever do something like that?"

"Of course not!" she denied indignantly, meeting his gaze directly for the first time since he'd arrived.

"That's good."

She looked away again, unable to maintain the eye contact. "But I'm afraid…I'm afraid Heather might be tempted."

"No, she wouldn't. Heather has her head screwed on straight, believe me."

His unquestioning faith in Heather annoyed Sam. How could he be so blind? "Are you sure you know her as well as you think you do?"

"Are you implying that I don't?"

She wished she could read his expression. He looked so cool, so remote. "Well…she's said a few things to me that have made me think that there might be a few problems."

He frowned. "What kind of problems?"

Sam tried to think of one that would grossly offend him. "Um, well…sexual problems."

"Sexual problems?"

"She…well, she said you're a terrible kisser."

He made a choking noise, turning his face away. Sam couldn't tell if he was angry or hurt. He was very quiet for a long time. She leaned forward, trying to see his expression, and detected a slight furrow on his brow, as if he was thinking hard.

"I know this is a sensitive subject, but I thought you should know."

He turned back and looked at her for a long moment. Something about his gaze made her shift uncomfortably. "Yes, it is something I should know. And I must believe you because I know you would never lie to me about such a thing."

Sam averted her gaze and shifted uneasily again. "Uh, no."

"Hmm." He stroked his chin. "There's only one solution that I can see."

"Oh?" she asked, hope rising in her. Was he going to break off the engagement? Or at least delay the wedding? "What's that?"

"I'm going to have to get someone to teach me how to kiss." His gaze turned toward hers. "Sam, I hate to ask you, but would you help me out here?"

"Me? You can't be serious!"

"I know it will be difficult," he said. "Especially since I feel absolutely no sexual attraction for you. But no matter how unpleasant it will be for me to kiss you, I'm willing to do it if it will help me with Heather."

Sam frowned. Surely kissing her wouldn't be *that* unpleasant. Did he have to sound like such a martyr? She opened her mouth to say no, she wouldn't kiss him if he were Brad Pitt, Ewan McGregor and Ben Affleck combined, but then remembered her plan. She was supposed to get him to kiss her. This was all working out perfectly. She couldn't let a little thing like pride stand in her way.

"Sam? Will you help me?"

She hesitated. Actually, she hadn't expected it to be quite so easy. She'd thought he would put up more of a fight. Didn't the thought of kissing someone other than the woman he loved make him feel guilty? But then again, why should it? He obviously was completely unattracted to Sam.

She glanced at him. His face was very solemn. Her gaze drifted down to his mouth. He had a nice mouth—firm lips, with a long thin upper lip and a shorter, fuller lower one....

He put his hand on her shoulder and she jumped.

"What's the matter?" he asked her.

"Nothing." His thumb was at the neckline of her dress, resting against her bare skin. "What time is it?"

"Ten-twenty. Why?"

"Oh...nothing." Ten minutes. Was it too early? Could she get him to kiss her for ten minutes? Taking a deep breath, she tilted her face up and closed her eyes. "Okay. Go ahead. Kiss me."

There was a small silence. His mouth didn't touch hers. He didn't speak.

She opened her eyelids halfway. He was staring down at her with an odd expression in his eyes. "Is something wrong?" she asked.

"No. Nothing," he said, but he still made no move to kiss her.

He must be feeling guilty, after all, she realized. Oh, no! Quickly, before he could tell her he'd changed his mind, she stood on tiptoe, put her arms around his neck and kissed him.

He tensed. His hands went up to her arms and she thought he was going to drag them from around his neck. He gripped her wrists tightly. Then, suddenly, his hands slid down her arms to her back, and down her back to her hips where they pulled her up tightly against him as his mouth opened up over hers.

For a moment, the darkness behind her eyelids was lit up with sparks that whirled around and around. She gasped, and he kissed her more deeply, his mouth sucking at her tongue in a way that caused the sparks to whirl faster. He kissed her like a drowning man seeking oxygen; like a starving man seeking sustenance; like a man in the desert seeking water.

And she...she found herself clinging to him, as breathless, hungry and thirsty as he was. She wanted the kiss to go on and on. She hadn't realized a kiss could be like this. She didn't want it to stop....

His mouth lifted from hers. "How was that?" he murmured against her lips.

"It...it was fine," she managed to say.

"C'mon, Sammy. I need you to be honest with me. Do you think I need to do something else?" He kissed her cheek, her ear. "Should I talk to her? Tell her that she smells like the sweetest honeysuckle, that she tastes like honey and red wine? That touching her, holding her, makes me feel drunk, dizzy, dazed...?"

His words brushed over her skin like butterfly wings. She was melting inside, a sluggish, heavy lava spreading through her veins. "I...I suppose that would be okay."

"Can I tell her that I think about her all day, all night? That seeing her, looking at her, makes me sweat, that the sound of her voice, the touch of her hand, makes me want her? That I dream about her lying in my bed? I don't want to scare her. I just want to touch her...."

His hand skimmed down her back, a long, sensuous sweep, and settled on her buttocks again. "I want to hold her tight against me and let her feel what she does to me."

She *could* feel it. The hard ridge pressed against her stomach. She wished she was taller. She wished it was pressing lower, where the aching, melting yearning was.

"Tell me what I should do now, Sammy," he murmured. "Tell me how to please you...."

Involuntarily, she squirmed against him and she heard him groan. His hands moved to her waist, his breathing harsh in her ear.

"Sammy..."

There was a sudden hesitation in his voice. He was going to push her away, she thought with a stabbing, piercing fear. He was going to push her away and she couldn't bear it if he did. She arched her back, pressing her breasts against his chest.

"Sammy..." His grip tightened around her waist. "Aw, hell," he muttered, then covered her mouth with his. He picked her up and set her on the edge of the table on top of the satin she'd unrolled. It felt slick and cool under her heated skin. He moved between her knees, causing her legs to splay wide, and pressed himself up against the exact spot she'd wanted him to.

"God, Sammy. I'd forgotten...how you can make me insane...." He nibbled the side of her neck. "Tell me what I should do next. Should I touch you like this?" His hand moved up to cup her breast. "And this?" His other hand stroked the inside of her thighs. "I want to kiss your nipples and your stomach and in between your legs. I want you so much. I've wanted you forever...."

His fingers moved up her thigh and touched silk.

She gulped in air. "Brad...I...I..." She needed to tell him something. But she couldn't think. Didn't want to think. She only wanted him to keep doing what he was doing. She wanted the pleasure to continue. She wanted...she wanted...

She cried out, shudders racking her, sending her

spiraling. She sagged against him, breathless, stunned. She couldn't believe...she hadn't realized...who would have thought Brad could make her feel such pleasure? Brad, her dearest, most wonderful friend...

Her *friend*.

Oh, dear God!

She stiffened, her blood suddenly turning cold.

"Shh," he murmured against her hair. "It's all right, Sam. It's all right—"

"No, it's not!" She could barely speak. "Let go of me!"

He held her more tightly. "What's the matter, Sam? Don't you like it when I touch you like this?"

The sensations were returning, building, more intense than before. Oh, dear heaven. She *did* like it. She liked it too much. She grabbed his wrist and pulled at his hand.

For a moment, he resisted, and she thought he was going to ignore her. But then, slowly, reluctantly, he put his hand back on her waist and looked down at her. "What's the matter, Sammy?"

She couldn't meet his gaze. "Nothing. I...I...what time is it?"

He kissed her lips possessively. "Who the hell cares?"

She pushed at his shoulders. "I care! What time is it?"

"It's ten-forty-five. Why?"

Ten-forty-five. Where was Kristin?

"No reason." She started to shake. What had happened to her? She'd been kissed before. But before, there had always been a small, detached corner of her brain monitoring what was going on and signaling when things were getting out of hand.

But tonight the signal hadn't been there. He could have pushed her back against the table and had sex with her instead of just petting her and she wouldn't have stopped him. She'd been out of control, something that had never happened to her before. What was wrong with her? This wasn't supposed to happen....

She got off the table and stepped away from him, straightening her dress with trembling hands. "I think you'd better leave now."

He reached out toward her. "Sammy...everything's okay. Don't look so upset. I didn't mean to frighten you. I got a little carried away—"

"A little!" She turned away from him, crossing her arms across her chest. "This was wrong."

"Was it?"

She cast a quick glance at him. His eyes were still dark from passion. Her heart thumped in response, and she averted her gaze quickly. What had happened? How had he made her lose all rational thought, all sense of herself, to become totally engulfed by him? How could he have done that to her? Especially when he was supposedly in love with Heather....

Heather.

"You don't love Heather, do you?" she asked urgently, putting her hand on his arm. "You couldn't love her and...and kiss me like that. You can't marry her. It's probably a good thing this happened. Better that you know now than after the wedding. Don't be too upset. I'm sure you'll find someone else in time."

His arm stiffened under her fingers. "Someone? Like who?"

"I…I don't know." Her hand dropped to her side. "Someone who loves you and cares about you. Heather never did."

He stared at her, his face full of…disbelief? Disappointment? Anger? "Forget about Heather. Let's talk about *you*. What *you* felt a few minutes ago. You did feel something, didn't you, Sam?"

"I…I…"

"Come on, admit it. For once in your life, admit the truth."

She stepped back. "I don't know what you're talking about—"

"Yes, you do." He came after her, backing her up against the dress rack. Hangers pressed into her shoulders, full, lacy skirts billowed around her. "Admit it, Sam. That there's an attraction between us, that there's always been an attraction between us, but you were too damned scared to own up to it. That you ran off to New York and then Europe rather than acknowledge it."

"You're crazy," she whispered. "There was nothing between us—"

"Wasn't there? Then tell me, why did you leave without saying goodbye?"

"You weren't home, you were on a business trip…it was a spur-of-the-moment decision, an impulse…."

"Yeah, sure. The whole month before you had your 'impulse,' you jumped every time I touched you, you blushed every time I looked at you—"

"I don't know what you're talking about," she said again through tight lips. "We were friends, nothing more. You must have been imagining it."

He stepped back and thrust his fists into his pock-

ets. "Okay. If that's the way you want it. I was imagining it. And *you* were imagining whatever you
thought was going on tonight. I was simply trying to
improve my kissing technique for Heather's sake. It
meant as little to me as it did to you. It *didn't* mean
anything to you, correct?"

"I…no, of course not." It hadn't…had it? Brad
was her friend. But he didn't seem like her friend
anymore. Everything had changed. *He* had changed.
Where had he learned to kiss like that? To touch like
that? It was the last thing she would have expected
from him. She would have expected him to be gentle
and considerate, not forceful and assertive. How could
he have changed so much? And why was he looking
at her like that? Like he wanted to throttle her. Like
he *hated* her.

Her throat was so tight, she could barely breathe.

"Good." He gave her a frozen smile. "Then I'd
better be on my way."

He strode toward the door and Sam stood there
helplessly, her thoughts and emotions in turmoil. She
felt wobbly, as if she were wearing the in-line skates.
She felt confused, as if she was lost in the maze again.
Only one thought was clear—he was leaving. He was
leaving, and she sensed that if she didn't stop him, if
she let him go, then she would lose him forever.

"Brad," she called after him. "Wait…"

Ignoring her, he flung open the door.

"Wait, Brad…"

He stopped abruptly, and for a moment, she
thought he was listening to her. But then she saw the
two women on the front doorstep.

Kristin, her hand lifted to grasp the knob, stood
motionless, her eyes wide and her mouth hanging open.

The other woman's cool gaze traveled down over Samantha's disheveled clothes. She turned to Brad.

"Oh, Brad!" Heather said, her voice tragic. "How could you?"

Chapter Ten

"The antitrust issues are all settled and the final paperwork should be done today. Disbursements can start next week." George Yorita opened the file in his hand and glanced at the contents. "I had Lewis work out the precise formula based on each employee's length of employment plus his salary. It comes out to an average of $58,000 per person and...for God's sake, Brad, what the hell's the matter with you?"

Brad turned his gaze away from his office window and the car crash on the 405 freeway twenty stories below him, glancing over his shoulder at his business partner and friend. "Nothing's the matter."

George snorted as he tossed the file onto Brad's desk. The papers inside skidded out and across the polished oak until they ran up against the base of a gold-plated statuette. "Come on. I've been in your office three times today and you haven't polished your trophy once. So what's the deal? Having trouble with your *fiancée?*"

Brad ignored the sarcastic edge on the last word. "Heather's fine." He gave his friend a level look. "I know what I'm doing, George."

"Yeah, right." George's black eyes snapped and his thick brows met in the middle of his forehead. He headed for the door, then paused. "You know, it might work if you just told her how you feel."

George left, his back stiff, and Brad sighed. He and George went way back. The two of them had competed in high school for the best grades in math and the most points in tennis. They'd been typical teenage guys, not much for verbalizing their feelings, but they had talked about girls. George'd had several volatile relationships before settling down with Laura. Brad liked and respected him more than anyone he knew, but in this particular case, George was dead wrong....

Brad turned his gaze back to the window. Far below, an ambulance was speeding down the shoulder toward the crash, passing the creeping traffic, red lights flashing. The siren was muted by the thick glass, but still audible.

A similar alarm had gone off in his head last night when he'd entered the bridal shop. Seeing Sam in that transparent dress, smelling the heady scent of her, he'd known he was in trouble. Recklessly, he'd ignored his instincts, telling himself that he could stay in control, but he'd damned well nearly lost it. He'd known he shouldn't kiss her. Not then, not like that. But he hadn't been able to resist. He'd wanted to kiss her since she was fourteen years old, and last night, finally, he'd had the opportunity. Who could blame him for grasping it—and her—with both hands?

He remembered the day he'd met her as if it were yesterday. He'd been just about to give that ass Pete

Mitchell an explicit, two-word suggestion what to do with himself, when she'd pounced, bristling like a baby porcupine. He'd only been able to see her back and a stubby black ponytail as she'd laid into Pete, calling him a jerk and a bully and threatening to tell his mother what had *really* happened to her prized antique perfume bottles if he didn't back off.

Pete had slunk away, and Brad, annoyed by her interference, had been about to tell her to go home and play with her Barbie dolls, when she'd turned and smiled up at him.

Something had squeezed in his heart. She'd been so damned beautiful. Big green eyes flecked with gold, pale skin sprinkled with freckles that looked like brown sugar. The top of her tousled curls barely reached his shoulder, but her cheerleader's outfit had revealed surprising long legs and damned sweet breasts. At seventeen, still hormone-driven, he'd gone instantly hard, but at least he'd held on to his wits enough to hide it. She'd looked way too young for him.

That belief was confirmed when he found out she was fourteen. He'd been determined to ignore her, but she'd turned out to be as persistent as a gnat. She'd stopped by his locker, plopped down next to him at lunch, tagged after him on the walk home from school, chattering about school, her friends and her family. She'd made him smile for the first time since his parents and Molly had been killed in a car accident on the way home from the sixth-grade class's promotion ceremony.

He'd let down his guard enough that he'd told Sammy about his little sister one day. Molly had been six years younger than him and a pest. Most of the time he'd tolerated her following him around, but one morning, after a sleepless night spent studying for a calculus final, he'd gotten fed up and snapped at her to get lost. Several hours later, in the middle of the test, the principal, tears in her eyes, had come to his class and asked him to come to the office.

He hadn't cried then, and he didn't cry when he told Samantha—although she wept enough for both of them—but that night, when he went back to his grandmother's and lay in the dark in his hard, narrow bed, the knot in his chest, the one that had been there for the last six months, started expanding. It grew and grew until he could barely breathe, and a hoarse sob had escaped him. And then another, and another, until his throat and chest ached and his face and pillow were wet with tears. Afterward, he'd felt drained, exhausted and faintly embarrassed by his lack of control, but he'd slept better that night than he had in a long time, and he woke up feeling lighter—and hopelessly, inescapably in love with Sammy.

He'd tried to tell himself that she reminded him of his kid sister and treated her accordingly. But deep in a corner of his heart, he knew he was waiting—waiting for her to grow up so he could marry her.

But things didn't work out the way he planned. In the next few years her parents divorced, her sister married hastily, her father passed away. The combination of events worked against him, making her extremely wary of men. She changed boyfriends as often as she bought a new dress. She dropped every boy who pressured her, and he'd known that if he hinted at anything more than friendship, he would suffer the same fate. He just had to be patient, he'd thought.

She would get over her skittishness and then he would have a chance.

But to his frustration, she'd been completely satisfied with a friendly relationship and continued to shy away from anything deeper, from the slightest suggestion of anything the least bit sexual. He'd waited until he couldn't wait any longer, and then he'd started a subtle campaign to change the status quo.

With a casual hug here, a brush of the fingers there, he'd tried to break through her barriers, make her more aware of him. It had worked, too—so well that he'd even bought a house and taken her to see it. He'd thought she would love it. And she had, he'd seen it in her eyes.

But a few days later, she left for New York.

He'd decided to wash his hands of her, to get on with his own life. And he had. He'd built up his business, met other women. He'd told himself he was over her, that he could stop himself from loving her.

Yeah, right. He could stop himself from loving her the way Pavlov's dogs could stop themselves from salivating.

Last night she'd kissed him, she'd responded to him, the way he'd dreamed of. Kissing Sammy, touching her, had been a lightning-charged, fuse-popping experience. But the aftermath had been more like a rolling blackout.

Her words couldn't have been more insulting, more uncaring. Thank God Heather had showed up when she did. She'd been a trouper. He'd explained the situation to her, but he wouldn't have been surprised if she'd found it just too damn much and called the whole thing off. Instead, she'd insisted that she understood. She was an amazing woman—kind and sympathetic and unbelievably good-natured. He'd felt a savage satisfaction, seeing Sam's face as he walked out of the shop with Heather on his arm. But the feeling had faded quickly.

Brad watched as two stretchers were carried to the ambulance. He had to stop fooling himself. Stop pretending he could have everything he wanted. Life didn't work that way, and he should know it better than anyone. Cars crashed. People died. And you couldn't make a woman love you, no matter how much you wanted her to.

He turned away from the window and sat down at his desk, gathering the papers back into the file George had thrown down. It was time to face the facts and move on. Sam would never love him. He had to forget about her.

The phone rang. He picked it up and his assistant's voice came across the line.

"Samantha Gillespie is on line three," Marilyn told him. "Do you want to talk to her?"

Brad stared at the blinking light.

I'm sure you'll find someone else in time.

"No," he said in a hard voice. "Tell her I'm busy."

He hung up the phone and stared down at the file, scanning the columns of figures. The amounts looked reasonable. Lewis had done a good job. So had George. He was going to have to explain to George—

The phone rang again.

"Yes?" he snapped into the phone.

"I'm sorry," Marilyn said. "But Ms. Gillespie asked me to give you a message. She said she needed to talk to you. She wants you to meet her at the restaurant across the street at noon. She said she'll wait for you.''

What the hell did she want now? ''Call her back and tell her I can't make it,'' he ordered, then paused. ''No, wait. Never mind. I'll take care of it myself.''

He disconnected, his brow furrowing as he stared at the RiversWare Run trophy on his desk. The engraved silver cup listed the names of the winners for the past five years. His name was listed for the last three years.

He dialed a number. The phone rang a couple of times before a feminine voice answered. ''Hello?''

''Hi, Heather, this is Brad.'' Holding the phone between his neck and shoulder, he opened a desk drawer and pulled out a rag. He picked up the trophy and wiped it with the cloth, rubbing at a tiny speck of tarnish. ''Could you do me a favor?''

Sam sat in the restaurant booth, pretending to sip her drink and glancing at her watch every few seconds. It was almost twelve-thirty. She'd gotten there early, at eleven-thirty, to make sure she didn't miss him.

Where was he?

Sam poked at the strawberry in her lemonade with a straw. He couldn't stand her up. She needed to talk to him. She needed to make sense of what had happened at the shop.

If that were at all possible.

That kiss had shaken her to her very foundation. Even so, she might have been able to laugh it off, dismiss it as an aberration, if it weren't for Brad's behavior afterward. He'd been furious, and he'd accused her of...of what, exactly?

She didn't know. All she knew was that he was her friend and she didn't want that to change. If it did, everything would be different. Different and scary. He'd been the one constant in her life the past ten years, the one person she could cling to when the world was falling apart around her. She didn't want to lose that. And yet…and yet…

She couldn't get the memory of the way he'd kissed her out of her head. And touched her…oh, dear heaven, the way he had touched her! She wished…she wished she could have talked to him. But Heather had arrived, making that impossible. Heather, who hadn't even cared that her fiancé had obviously been kissing another woman. Oh, the blonde had ranted and cried enough to be the heroine of a melodrama, but Sam had heard the false ring in the blonde's hollow words, seen the calculating gleam in the blue eyes when Brad promised to "make it up" to her.

Brad was oblivious though. Sam had wanted to shout at him. Couldn't he see Heather was only interested in his money? Couldn't he see the way her tears had stopped so quickly and easily and the sly smile on her lips when he told her that Sam meant nothing to him, that Sam was like a little sister to him, a friend, nothing more?

Sam frowned down at her strawberry. She'd said something similar herself countless times. There was no reason for those words to sting so sharply. Hearing them should have made her happy, should have relieved her. But they hadn't. She'd felt strangely betrayed, as though he'd plunged a dagger into her heart.

She'd told herself that it was only because she was

worried about a dear friend, but her self-assurances had rung as hollow as Heather's protestations of love for Brad. Something had changed about her feelings for Brad. Her emotions were all messy, crazy, mixed-up. She needed to talk to him about it. She needed to find out...she needed to know...she needed to ask him if he felt something, too....

"Waiting for someone?"

Sam's head snapped up at the mocking voice and she stared in horror at the woman standing by the booth.

Heather! In a gold pantsuit, the jacket unbuttoned to reveal generous cleavage and a diamond necklace, the blonde looked absolutely stunning.

"You don't mind if I join you, do you?" Heather asked as she slid into the opposite seat.

"Uh, actually, I *am* waiting for...for someone," Sam stammered.

"Oh, yes, I know. Brad told me all about your pitiful little call. He got caught up in a meeting this morning, so he asked me to come and explain." She crooked a finger, and a waiter magically appeared. "I'll have the Thai chicken pizza, salad and iced tea."

Reeling from the knowledge that Brad had told Heather about her phone call, Sam set the menu aside without looking at it. "I'm just having lemonade," she said, feeling sick inside. The waiter left, and Sam, not looking at Heather, said, "Thanks for passing on Brad's message. I guess I better go. Here's some money for the lemonade—"

"Don't rush off." Heather waved aside the five-dollar bill Sam held out. "I want to talk to you."

"What about?"

"Don't give me that innocent look." The blonde

put a cigarette in her mouth and took out her lighter in spite of the prominently displayed No Smoking signs. "I want to know what you're up to."

Sam stared down at her lemonade. "I don't know what you mean."

Heather put her elbows on the table and leaned forward, the unlit cigarette dangling from her lips. "Listen, you don't fool me one bit. You're hot for him, aren't you? You were trying to get him to have sex with you at the shop last night, weren't you?"

"No!" The denial was instinctive and involuntary. Sam's face burned.

"Oh, please. You think I don't recognize a female in heat? You couldn't have been more obvious."

Sam gulped some lemonade, trying to cool her hot skin. "You're wrong."

"I'm never wrong when it comes to sizing up the competition. Not that you're much of an opponent. In fact, you're more of a help than a hindrance. I probably should be thanking you."

Sam looked into the blonde's cool eyes. "For what?"

"For that little stunt at the shop, of course. Brad felt terribly guilty. He was pathetically grateful for my forgiving him and trusting him and went all out to make it up to me." Heather stroked the diamond necklace. "Anytime you want to make a pass at him, be my guest."

Sam clutched the napkin on her lap, crumpling it into a tiny ball. The actress was the most despicable person she'd ever met. Brad deserved so much more. He deserved someone who appreciated him, who understood him, who loved him wholeheartedly....

"There's something you should know," Sam said,

then paused as the waiter delivered Heather's food. She tried to think of something to say. Something calm and cool, that would inform Heather that Sam would not allow the blonde to go through with this wedding. That she wouldn't allow Heather to destroy Brad's life.

But looking at Heather's composed face and derisive eyes, Sam couldn't seem to force the words to her lips. She had a terrible feeling the other woman would laugh at her. Panic and desperation welled up in Sam.

"There's something I should know?" Heather prompted.

"Yes, you should know..." Sam took a deep breath, then blurted out, "Brad snores!"

Heather put the unlit cigarette back in her purse and picked up a piece of pizza. "That will give me a great excuse to have separate bedrooms. I was planning on claiming he snored even if he didn't."

"That's not all." Sam sipped her lemonade, giving herself time to think of something else. "He has a fetish for wearing women's dresses!"

Heather yawned. "So?"

Sam swallowed. "I just thought you should know. Some women might not understand—"

"Listen, Sam, I'm an actress. I'm used to all kinds of people and all kinds of little personality quirks. I can handle it."

"Uh, good," Sam said. "But there's something else."

"Yes?"

"He...he's a premature ejaculator!"

For the first time the blonde looked taken aback. "I'm sure I can handle him—er, that is..." Heather regained her composure. "He hasn't had that problem with me at all."

It took a second for the implication of Heather's words to sink in. When they did, Sam blanched. "What do you mean? I thought you and Brad hadn't..." She couldn't go on.

Heather paused a moment, as if considering her words carefully. Then she gave a tinkling laugh. "Did Brad tell you that? He's so old-fashioned, he was probably trying to protect my reputation. I slept with him a month ago. I must say, I was amazed by how *adept* he was."

Sam felt sick. So. They had slept together. She felt like crying.

Heather laughed again. "Brad even believed me when I told him I was a virgin. That's how I got him to propose."

Suddenly, Sam didn't feel like crying anymore. Her fingers curled into claws. She wanted to scratch Heather's eyes out. She wanted to yank huge clumps of shining blond hair out by the roots....

"Then there's something else you should know," Sam heard herself say. "Last night Brad made love to *me.*"

Heather's brows rose. "My dear, please don't embarrass yourself any further. If Brad wants to keep a slut on the side, I'm certainly not going to object."

A *slut!* Sam's fingers closed around her glass of lemonade as she fought the nearly irresistible urge to dump its contents over the blonde's perfectly coiffed head—

"Look, Samantha," Heather said, leaning back in her seat. "Let's cut all the crap. Why don't you just admit that you want Brad for yourself."

"Because it's not true."

Heather snorted. "Lie if you want, it doesn't matter to me. Even though Brad had a crush on you once, he's well over it, believe me."

"Brad had a crush on me?" Sam blurted out the question before she could prevent herself.

"Don't pretend you didn't know," Heather said. "But that's all water under the bridge. He loves *me* now. Your telling him that you love him won't make any difference."

Love? She wasn't in love with Brad. At least...

"Brad and I are friends," she said, whether to herself or to the blonde, she wasn't sure.

"Oh, come on," Heather said. "Just admit it. Admit that you're in love with him."

Sam stared into the blonde's relentless blue eyes, unable to speak, her stomach suddenly twisting into knots. In her head, she heard Brad's voice, his words eerily similar to the blonde's.

Admit it. For once in your life, admit the truth.

Sam's skin felt clammy. Oh, dear heaven...

"Excuse me," a male voice snarled.

Sam looked up to see a black-haired man looming over them. Startled, she drew back a little, then realized all his attention was focused on Heather.

"Ms. Lovelace, may I have a word with you?"

"N-no. I'm busy."

Sam looked at Heather in surprise. Underneath her faux tan, the other woman was pale to her lips and she was actually shrinking back in her seat. Sam had never seen her look so frightened.

"I think you'd better come with me—if you know what's good for you. Although I would be glad to have our conversation here, in front of your friend."

Heather looked as though she might faint.

In spite of herself, Sam's protective instincts rushed to the fore. No matter how much she hated Heather, she wouldn't sit by and see the woman terrorized. "Sir," she said, straightening her spine. "Please go away or I'll call the manager."

For the first time the man looked at her. Sam shivered a little under the bright icy blue of his eyes. Then he looked back at Heather. "Well?"

Heather's lips curved into a strained smile. "Samantha, we'll have to finish our conversation some other time. Excuse me."

Frowning, Sam watched Heather walk away with the strange man. Heather walked stiffly, not with her usual hip-swinging stride. Sam didn't quite know what to think. Heather was obviously reluctant, but she also obviously knew the man. Who was he? And why did he appear so angry? Would he try to hurt Heather?

Sam got up from the table and went over to the windows by the front door. Peering out, she saw the man and Heather standing in the parking lot. The man was waving his arms threateningly.

Sam opened the door and went outside. She scurried over behind a palm tree and glanced warily around the edge. If the man tried to hurt Heather, Sam planned to scream for help at the top of her lungs—

"You big lug, why don't you mind your own business!" Heather snarled at the man.

Startled, Sam ducked back behind the palm. She'd never heard Heather sound so *emotional* before.

"It *is* my business. This could affect your work."

"Is that all you care about, my work? For the last

time, *go away.* I never want to see you again, you selfish, egotistical—"

"Miss…"

Sam jumped and turned to see the waiter from the restaurant frowning at her. Quickly, she straightened. "I, uh, was just admiring the palm tree. I'm thinking of relandscaping my yard and this would be perfect—"

"You didn't pay your bill," he interrupted.

"Oh," she said, rather blankly. She fished through her purse, pulled out a credit card and held it out to him.

He stared at her as though she were a cherry short of a jubilee. "Aren't you going to come back inside?"

"Um, no. I, er, I'm waiting for someone. Could you please just bring the check out here for me to sign?"

He mumbled something, took her card and went back inside.

Cautiously, Sam peered around the tree again. Heather and the man were still arguing. The stranger had braced his arms against his car, Heather trapped between them.

"You're going to have to be careful while you're pregnant." he said. "I'll speak to the director—"

"I'm only a month along, you idiot. It will be months before it affects my work…."

Sam froze behind the palm tree.

Heather was *pregnant?*

Chapter Eleven

Sam stood in front of an ironing board in her living room that evening, carefully pressing her bridesmaid gown and trying desperately not to cry.

Brad was getting married tomorrow and there was nothing she could do to stop him.

She'd spent all afternoon and most of the evening trying to think of some other solution, some way to stop the wedding and salve her conscience, too. She'd had visions of offering to adopt the baby, to raise it as her own. But the rest of the conversation she'd overheard had made it clear that Heather would never agree to that.

"Have you told Rivers?" the stranger had asked Heather.

"Not yet. I'm going to tell him on our wedding night. He'll be delighted. He wants children."

"As much as you do?" the stranger had sneered at Heather.

"Don't laugh," Heather had retorted. "I may not

have wanted a baby, but I'm going to be the best mother possible.''

''You expect me to believe you care more about this baby than your ambition?''

''I don't care what you believe.'' Sam had never heard the blonde so resolute. ''I may have said some things in the past...but now I realize some things are more important than an acting career....''

The waiter had returned with the bill at that moment, and by the time Sam had signed the credit slip, Heather and the stranger had left the parking lot.

Sam spritzed one of the gown's pink ruffles, the terrible truth striking her once again. Heather was pregnant. *Pregnant!* With Brad's baby. And that fact seemed to have totally changed the blonde's perspective. She'd told the stranger she was going to be the best mother possible, that there were things more important than a career.

Maybe Heather was lying, Sam thought desperately as she pressed the ruffle with the iron. But she didn't think so. The blonde had sounded too sincere.

And if Heather truly cared about this baby, then Sam knew she had to back off. She knew it would be the utter height of selfishness to try to break up the couple when a baby was involved.

Sam gripped the iron. She had to stop trying to prevent the wedding. If she was truly Brad's friend, then that's what she had to do—even if she didn't want to be his friend anymore. Because at lunch, she'd finally realized the truth. She'd discovered the secret to the maze, and all the paths had led to one inescapable conclusion—she loved Brad.

She loved him.

She'd loved him for a long time, but she'd refused

to admit it. Subconsciously, though, she'd known it since that summer when she'd run away to New York. She'd been standing in the back yard of her mother's house, politely listening as Dave pointed out the tiny avocados on the tree in front of them, when Brad had joined them. She'd looked up into his laughing eyes and almost started laughing herself. But then he'd draped a casual arm around her shoulders and suddenly, unexpectedly, her heartbeat had doubled and she hadn't been able to breathe.

She'd tried to dismiss it as a fluke, but it had happened again the next day, when he'd put his hand on the small of her back to guide her across the street. And then again when he'd tucked a protruding tag into her collar at the back of her neck. There'd been other small touches, insignificant touches that she'd never noticed before, but now made her pulse flutter and her cheeks grow warm.

Then he'd bought a house.

She could still picture his house as she'd first seen it—Spanish tile, iron grillwork and a small courtyard with a fountain. She'd fallen in love with it immediately. And when he'd asked her if she would decorate it for him, she should have jumped at the chance. In fact, when he'd asked her, she'd been standing in the master bedroom, picturing how it would look with a carved four-poster bed, piled high with blankets and pillows and an old oak chest at the foot. She should have said yes, but somehow the words had stuck in her throat. The room had seemed very quiet and still, the only sound the slight creak of the polished floorboards. He'd been smiling at her, his eyes the same gray-blue as the ocean visible through the curtainless windows, and suddenly something had squeezed at her heart. Something so unexpected and so intense she'd barely been able to breathe. It hadn't been until he'd taken her home and she was alone in her own room that the constriction in her chest had eased.

She'd been frightened and embarrassed by her reaction and, fool that she was, she panicked. She'd seen what her parents and sister had gone through. She'd seen how love and passion could turn to hate and she hadn't wanted to end up like them. When Maria Vasquez had invited her to go to New York, Sam had run off rather than acknowledge that something had changed, that her feelings for Brad weren't purely friendly any longer.

And Brad…what about him? What had he felt? Heather had said he'd had a crush on Sam, but she'd never seen any sign of it. That day in his house, his expression had been friendly, but had there been something more? She didn't think so. He'd never said anything, never once kissed her. At least, not until last night.

That kiss…how could he kiss her and touch her like that and feel nothing but friendship for her? Why would he press her to "admit the truth"? Surely he must feel something. Some spark that had endured in spite of his engagement to another woman. If things were different, she could try to fan that spark. If Heather wasn't having his baby…

But Heather was.

She felt sick. She felt as if she was going to throw up. She'd been afraid that love would make her lose Brad's friendship. She hadn't realized that denying her feelings would cause her to end up losing him completely.

She loved Brad, but it was too late. He *had* to marry Heather....

A knock sounded at her door. Sniffling a little, she glanced at the clock. It was almost nine. Who would be coming to her apartment so late? One of her sisters, maybe. She wished they would go away. She didn't want to talk to anyone. She was too miserable.

The knock came again, louder this time. ''Sammy? Are you in there?''

Sam set down the iron. *Brad?*

She walked over to the door, tightening the belt of her Chinese silk robe. She looked through the peephole.

An oblong Brad stood on her porch.

She opened the door a crack and peered out at him. He was dressed in jeans and a faded T-shirt, his hair sticking up on end. Dark stubble shaded his chin. He looked dangerously attractive. ''What are you doing here?'' she gasped.

''Let me in,'' he ordered.

The authority in his voice made her obey automatically. Once inside, he turned and stared at her.

Her insides quivered. Stifling a mad impulse to throw herself into his arms, she returned to the ironing board and picked up the iron. ''What are you doing? You shouldn't be here.''

He raked his fingers through his hair. ''I know.'' He thrust his hands in his pockets, watching her iron the gown. ''Heather called me. She thought...'' He paused, searching for words. ''You had lunch with her today.''

Sam pressed the same ruffle she'd pressed before he arrived. ''I was surprised when she turned up instead of you.''

"I'm sorry about that. It was just that I was angry about last night."

Sam stared down at the bright pink material under the iron. He had reason to be angry. She'd failed him. In more ways than one. "I'm sorry, too," she said. "It was all my fault."

"No, it wasn't," he contradicted her. "It was mine. I knew...that is, I shouldn't have lost my temper—"

"Please, Brad." She set the iron on its end and gave him a strained smile. "Let's pretend it never happened. Okay? Don't let it spoil your wedding."

A frown knit his brow. "My wedding. You know, Sam, I've been thinking, perhaps I should postpone the wedding—"

"No, Brad, you can't do that. Heather is counting on you."

"Sam." He walked over to her and took her elbow, his voice tight. "I have to talk to you. I never meant for this to go so far. I don't love Heather—"

He didn't love Heather? Oh, dear heaven. For a moment, Sam felt as though she were floating on a silk parachute. But then she hit earth with a thud.

Heather. And her baby. How could Sam have forgotten even for a second?

"Brad, you're beside yourself," she interrupted, pulling away from him, her voice low and strained. "You don't know what you're saying. Of course you love Heather."

"No, I don't. Oh, damn, how can I ever explain—"

"There's no explanation necessary. She's a beautiful woman—"

He inhaled deeply. "Yes, she is. But do you think she's the right woman for me?"

No! Sam wanted to scream. *She's all wrong for you!* But she couldn't.

Her heart breaking, Sam smiled bravely at him. "Yes, Brad. I think she's the perfect woman for you."

"You do?" He looked rather stunned.

"Oh, yes! Absolutely! She…she's gorgeous, she cares about animals. What more could you want?"

"What more, indeed?" he murmured, staring at her as though he'd never seen her before. "What did you and Heather talk about at the restaurant today?"

"Nothing much." Sam fiddled with the setting on the iron. "I assured her that nothing happened between you and me."

"Nothing happened?" His voice had a sarcastic edge to it. "Is that how you describe that kiss? The way you shuddered when I put my fingers inside you?"

Sam looked away, her cheeks feeling as if she'd pressed them against the iron. "Please, Brad…"

"Please what? Please *you?* Because that's what I could have sworn I was doing last night. The way you pleased me." He put his hands on her shoulders. "God, Sam, kissing you, touching you, was sheer heaven. And you felt the same way. Didn't you?"

"N-no," Sam croaked.

Brad moved closer. "I talked to Heather. She said you…cared about me."

Sam felt frozen. She couldn't speak.

He stared down at her intently. "I can't stop thinking about last night, Sam. You felt so good in my arms. You tasted so sweet. I didn't want to stop. I wanted to keep on kissing you. I wanted to push you back against that satin and make love to you."

"Brad…"

"Yes, Sam? Tell me what you want. Tell me the truth. Tell me that you want me as much as I want you…."

Oh, God. How could she think straight when he was talking to her like this? How could she think at all? But she had to. She had to remember Heather— and the baby.

With a superhuman effort, she stepped away from Brad, breaking his hold on her. She forced the words from her lips. "I do want you…as a friend."

"A friend? That's it?"

Her heart breaking, she nodded.

Anger flashed across his face. "You're lying. Dammit, you almost let me make love to you. Heather was right. You would never have let me go so far if you didn't feel something for me."

"You discussed this with Heather?" Sam was horrified.

Brad seemed to check himself. "We had a discussion," he said carefully. "I told her I was having some doubts about our marriage—"

"No!" Sam cried out. "You must marry her!"

"I must?" Brad looked at her closely. "Why must I?"

She bit her lip. Heather had said she was going to tell him about the baby on their wedding night. Sam wanted to blurt out the truth, that she loved him, that Heather was pregnant, that he had to marry Heather for the baby's sake. But she knew it would be selfish of her to do so. Brad needed to go into this marriage with a clear conscience and a whole heart.

She managed a careless shrug. "You can do whatever you want, of course. It really doesn't make any difference to me one way or the other. I have my own life to take care of. I start classes next week—"

"You enrolled at the design institute?"

"Yes," she answered, not looking at him. "Thank you for talking to your friend about me. When I spoke to him, he told me what to expect and didn't pull any punches. It's not an easy profession to break into, but I know this is what I want to do and I'm going to work my tail off. I won't have time for anything else—"

"Not even love?"

Tears burned in her eyes again, but she blinked them back fiercely. She couldn't cry, not now. If she did, he would wrap his arms around her and hold her. That's what he'd always done in the past. But she couldn't let him do it now—she would break down if he did, and tell him everything.

She forced herself to laugh. "The last thing I need in my life is a man. Thanks to you, I finally know what I want to do and I plan to focus all my energy on my career."

"I see," he said, his face expressionless. "You obviously have your life all planned out. Excuse me, I don't know what I was thinking. I'll leave before I waste any more of your valuable time." He turned toward the door.

"Wait!" she burst out before she could prevent herself.

His hand on the knob, he looked over his shoulder. "What?" he asked curtly.

Sam bit her lip. "Are you going to marry Heather tomorrow or not?"

He stared at her a long moment. "Yes. I'm going through with it. Will that make you happy, Sam?"

"Yes...that is, my feelings have nothing to do with it."

"You've made that very clear." He opened the door. "Sorry I bothered you."

Without another word, he stalked out of the apartment, slamming the door behind him.

Sam burst into tears.

Sam arrived late at the Temple of Peace and Tranquility. The white marble edifice stood at the edge of a high cliff over the Pacific Ocean. Waves crashed against the rocks below, but the temple itself was surrounded by a green lawn and stately trees, and a pleasant breeze flowed across the grounds. The sun shone brightly, and even though rain would have suited her mood better, Sam was glad of the sun's vigor—she needed an excuse to wear her dark glasses to hide her red-rimmed eyes.

She walked slowly across the crowded lawn, instinctively looking for Brad. She saw no sign of him as she passed little clumps of people. They were huddled together, casting suspicious glances at the other groups.

"Did you see what that woman was wearing?" The words floated up from one huddle of women in business suits and knee-length dresses. "It was completely see-through!"

Sam passed another group, which consisted of several exotic-looking women wearing clinging dresses, ghoulish black-and-white eye makeup and various pierced body parts. They were glancing over their shoulders at the other clump of women. "Have you ever seen such a thicket of boring-looking people in your life?" one woman said, twirling the end of her feather boa. "But what else can you expect from a bunch of people who live behind the Orange Curtain—"

"*There* you are!" Jeanette appeared out of nowhere, her temper obviously not matching the sunny yellow dress Sam had finally convinced her sister to let her make. "Where have you been? You're the maid of honor—you're supposed to be with Heather."

"Sorry," Sam muttered.

"Good grief, Samantha. It would be nice if once—just once!—you would make the effort to get somewhere on time. I've been going crazy here. The harpist brought the wrong music, the sprinklers drenched half the chairs—" Jeanette broke off suddenly, staring at Sam's face. "Are you all right?"

"I'm fine." Sam stretched her lips, attempting a smile.

Jeanette's voice grew hesitant. "Samantha…are you in love with Brad?"

"In love with Brad?" Sam forced herself to laugh. "Of course not."

"All this effort you've gone to to break up his engagement—"

"I was just worried about him. I've realized now that I was mistaken about Heather." Sam's throat ached as she spoke the words. "I want Brad to marry her."

Jeanette looked relieved. "That's good. To tell you the truth, I always did like her." Her tone became more brisk. "You'd better go to the temple. Heather, Audrey, Brendan and Cassie are already there. The ceremony is going to start in fifteen minutes. I'll be along shortly. I have to get the attendant to unlock the bathroom. And Sam—'' Jeanette's voice turned threatening. ''If you're late, I swear we'll start without you.''

Jeanette hurried off before Sam could answer. Not that Sam wanted to respond. She headed slowly toward the temple. Rows of chairs were on the grass, along with an altar decorated with white bows. She saw Audrey in pink gloves, stroking the skirt of her pink gown that matched Sam's but somehow looked adorable instead of tacky on her; Brendan in a small gray suit, jumping up and down as he tried to touch a low-hanging branch of the nearby oak tree; and Cassie, in frothy white lace, practicing throwing rose petals.

Sam was about to call out to them when she caught sight of Brad pacing on the other side of the temple. She stopped, staring at him hungrily.

He wore a stark black tuxedo, the clean lines accentuating the harsh angles of his face. He looked incredibly handsome...sexy. How could she have ignored that for so long? She wished she could go to him, explain everything, tell him how much she loved him....

He glanced up and saw her. His face hardening, he deliberately looked away.

Tears welled up in her eyes. Blindly, she turned away from the temple and hurried in the direction of a circle of trees. Once there, she tore off her sunglasses and wiped the tears from her cheeks with her handkerchief. If only she hadn't been such a fool. If only—

A muffled noise interrupted her thoughts. Peeking over a bush, she saw Heather—and the stranger from the parking lot. As Sam watched, the man grabbed Heather, hauled her into his arms and kissed her.

Shocked, Sam was about to jump out and yell at the man to stop, when she noticed that Heather didn't seem to be struggling. In fact, she appeared to be returning the kiss with amazing enthusiasm!

Sam stood frozen, unsure what to do. The man finally broke off the kiss, but only to pull Heather more tightly against him. He bent over her again, but Heather pulled away. "Stop, Joel! We can't do this. Brad—"

"Don't mention that name. You can't marry him, Heather, you can't. Especially not when you're carrying my baby…."

Sam gasped. The baby was *Joel's?*

"What else can I do?" Heather asked. Her hands trembling, she smoothed the white tulle skirt of her wedding dress. "You've made it plain *you* won't marry me. I've given you every possible chance to change your mind."

"Dammit, Heather, that's not fair…."

Heather pushed him away. "You're going to have to make up your mind one way or another, Joel. You have about five minutes to decide." She turned and ran in the direction of the temple.

Heather raced past, Joel following on her heels and arguing with her, but Sam barely noticed. Her brain was spinning. Joel's baby. The baby was *Joel's.* Heather must have been seeing the other man all along, behind Brad's back. Brad! Dear heaven, Brad didn't have to marry Heather. He *shouldn't* marry her. The blonde was deceiving him. The witch. The lying, conniving witch. How could she do this to Brad?

Brad, who was everything a woman could want in a man. A man who was strong, ethical, *honest*...

The strains of the wedding march drifted across the yard.

Sam gasped again. Grabbing her skirt, she ran through a wet swath of grass to where Audrey, Brendan and Cassie were just starting down the aisle. Quickly, she stepped behind them, her mind racing. She had to stop the wedding. But how? She didn't want to make a scene. She would have to try to say something to Brad at the altar. But would he believe her?

She walked down the aisle, barely aware of the rows of people, the scent of orange blossoms, the trilling of the harp. When she reached the altar, she looked at Brad. He stood straight and tall, but there was something cold and frozen about his face. His eyes appeared lifeless. He didn't look at her—not even a glance.

The minister, tall and bony with a brown beard that made him look a little like Jesus, raised his arms toward the sky. The full sleeves of his robe fluttered in the breeze. "Dearly beloved!" he boomed, making up in volume what he lacked in girth. He sounded more like he was preparing to deliver a sermon on hellfire and damnation than perform a marriage ceremony. "We are gathered here today to join this man and this woman...."

"Psst. Psst!" Sam hissed at Brad.

Heather, icy snow-queen perfection in her wispy silk gauze dress, turned her head and stared at Sam, but Brad didn't appear to hear her. He stared straight ahead, his face as cold as the temple's marble pillars.

She coughed, trying to get his attention. "Ahem. *Ahem.*"

Audrey thumped her on the back, almost knocking her over. Fred Calhoun, the best man, nudged Brad, but Brad didn't look away from the minister.

"In the holy bonds of matrimony," intoned the minister. "I repeat, the *holy bonds of matrimony.*"

Sam waved her bouquet at Brad. Cassie waved back at her, but Brad still didn't notice Sam.

"Samantha!" Sam heard her mother hiss from the front row of chairs. "Stop making a spectacle of yourself!"

Sam glanced over her shoulder. Sure enough, hundreds of eyes were staring at her—but Brad remained oblivious.

She began to despair as the minister continued the ceremony, his hands waving, his vocal chords quivering. What could she do? She must stop this wedding. She *must....*

"And now," the minister said, opening his arms wide, his voice crescendoing as though God Himself was speaking. "If there is *anyone here* who knows of *any reason why* this couple should *not wed,* let him *speak now,* or *forever hold his peace—*"

"I object!"

The shout drowned out Sam's croak. Startled, she looked over her shoulder and saw Joel, also on his feet.

"I object!" he said again.

Heather and Brad stood frozen. Sam heard her mother whisper to Dave, "Well, I never!" Other whispers and murmurings rose from the audience.

The minister did not look the least bit shocked or

surprised. In fact, he looked positively delighted. "On what grounds?" he thundered.

Joel stepped out into the aisle, knocking over a pot of lilies as he did so. Flowers and dirt spilled onto the walkway. "On the grounds that Heather Lovelace is carrying my child!"

Outraged gasps came from Brad's side of the congregation. Someone on Heather's side said "Ooeee! This keeps gettin' better 'n' better!"

Heather glared at Joel with burning eyes. "You just had to tell everyone, didn't you?" she said bitterly.

"Is this true?" Brad asked.

Heather hesitated, then nodded.

Suddenly, Brad looked straight at Sam. A frown knit his forehead. He stared, his gaze roving over her face, as if searching for something. Did he suspect she'd known? Was he wondering why she hadn't warned him?

Guiltily, she looked away.

When she glanced back, to her dismay, his face hardened. Apparently, he wasn't going to forgive her easily. He turned to Joel and studied him coolly a moment before taking Heather's hand in his. "I will still marry you," he said in a cold, hard voice. To the minister he said, "Please continue."

A roar thundered in Sam's ears; everything blurred. Last night Brad had said he didn't love Heather—but apparently that had been nothing more than prewedding jitters. He must love her if he was willing to marry her even though she was carrying another man's baby, even though she'd cheated on him. He must love her with all his heart and soul.

Sam felt as though she'd been hit in the stomach. She wanted to slink away. She wanted to hide. But she couldn't. Because she loved Brad. And she knew Heather didn't.

Her vision cleared. She became aware that the roaring in her ears was the sibilant whispers coming from the audience—and from Joel growling as he clenched and unclenched his fists.

The minister cleared his throat. "Then if there are no further objections…"

Sam clutched her bouquet. The news of Heather's pregnancy must have shocked Brad. Maybe he wasn't thinking clearly. Maybe, if he had time to think it over, he would realize he was making the biggest mistake of his life. Sam had to stop the ceremony. She *had* to…

"Brad and Heather, I now pronounce you—"

"Reverend, stop!" Sam burst out. "You can't marry this couple, because…because I'm pregnant also—with Brad's child!"

The volume of exclamations from the audience increased tenfold, the noise pierced by a loud wail from the front row. From the corner of her eye, Sam saw her mother slump onto Dave's shoulder, sobbing loudly into her handkerchief.

Brad's head swiveled in Sam's direction. He stared at her, not speaking. She stood tensely, wondering if he would denounce her as the liar she was.

The minister folded his arms across his chest. "These babies need parents. I can see only one solution. Joel, please come up here and stand next to Ms. Lovelace. And Brad, you move over next to Sam."

Brad tore his gaze away from Sam. "Reverend, I don't think this is a good idea…."

The minister waved his hand. "It's an excellent

idea. God will forgive your sins if you do the right thing now."

"I don't think it's *legal*," Brad said, an edge to his voice.

"It's perfectly legal." The minister waved a dismissive hand. "No blood tests are required when the parties have carnal knowledge of each other. And the licenses can be obtained after the fact if the situation is deemed an emergency. And I so deem."

"Reverend..." Brad said.

Sam's head was spinning again. She couldn't marry Brad—he didn't love her. He might not have denounced her, but he most certainly couldn't want to marry her. The only honorable thing to do was to refuse to go through with the ceremony....

But then he might insist on marrying Heather.

Sam took a deep breath and put her hand on his arm. "Please, Brad. I'll explain later, but for now, please marry me. For my mother's sake, if not mine."

He glanced at Vera, who was still moaning on Dave's shoulder, then back at Sam. His face darkened. His expression grew blacker and blacker.

He's going to refuse, she thought in dismay.

His eyes blazed. She half expected lightning to spring forth and strike her dead on the spot.

But instead, he reached out and pulled her tightly against his side. His voice, when he spoke, was grim.

"Continue, Reverend."

Chapter Twelve

What in heaven's name had she done?

The question was still revolving in Sam's brain several hours later as she walked dazedly through the crowded reception in a posh hotel, half listening to fragments of conversation around her.

"Where did you get those breasts done?" a red crushed-velvet vamp asked a floral-silk vice president of RiversWare.

"I have an excellent plastic surgeon," the woman responded. "He's in Newport Beach. I'll give you his name…"

"I made $1 million on my investments this year." A three-piece-suit, paisley-tie Asian gentleman pointed to the screen of his notebook computer.

"I made $10 million." A turbanned African-American male whipped out his own pocket computer and punched at the keys. "You have to watch out for those energy stocks…."

"I've been a corporate lawyer for thirty years,"

said a striped-bow-tie WASP. "But I've never heard of a minister having 'emergency powers.'"

"My specialty is entertainment law, not family law," responded a blue-sari lady in a wheelchair. "But I think I saw a movie once about a minister having emergency powers...."

Sam's smile felt plastic as she greeted people, most of them strangers, and accepted their congratulations. This wasn't how she'd pictured her wedding. Not that she'd imagined getting married very often, but she did remember the wedding Jeanette had planned for her when she was in the first grade. Maria Vasquez and Jessica Zangan, Sam's best friends, had been her bridesmaids. Quoc Ngo, the next-door kindergartner, had been the groom. All the kids on the block had come to watch the event. Sam had created a billowing dress out of her mother's old, slightly yellowed sheers, with a train that had dragged at least five feet behind her. Quoc had gazed at her adoringly as she tripped down the "aisle."

She'd never thought she would get married in a hideous pink gown, surrounded by mostly strangers, to a groom whose face looked like a block of ice whenever he glanced at her.

She avoided her family, but fortunately they didn't seem to notice. Dave and her mother sat at a table, happily eating slices of avocado off each other's forks; Audrey, Brendan and Cassie sat at another table, enthusiastically decorating their faces with fruit; Kristin and her boyfriend—a nice kid, Sam recalled—were quietly dancing on the dance floor. As were Jeanette, looking very beautiful in the yellow dress, and Matt, quite debonair in a brown suit and tie. They had their arms around each other, Jeanette's cheek resting on Matt's chest. They looked content. Marriage counseling must finally be working.

"Come on, let's get out of here," Brad growled in her ear.

Peeking at his face, she shivered. He was still angry at her, she could tell. And no wonder. She'd practically forced him to marry her. She'd done it because she loved him, but that was no excuse. Would he ever forgive her?

Judging by the cold look in his eyes, she doubted it.

"Wait," she protested weakly, trying to put off the inevitable. "We can't leave yet. We haven't talked to everyone—"

"No one will even notice," he said grimly, taking her elbow and leading her toward the elevator. "We've got a room on the twenty-second floor."

In spite of her resistance, he hustled her into the elevator, then paused, as if startled. Peering around his broad shoulders, she saw the two people she least wanted to see—Heather and Joel.

Sam saw that the light for floor twenty-two was already lit. Her spirits sank even lower. Was the couple going to be on the same floor?

Apparently so. The four of them stood silently as the elevator rose. Sam saw Brad and Heather exchange a glance. Her heart quivered. Were they wishing that they were riding up this elevator together—and alone?

Joel suddenly put his arm around Heather and held her tightly against his side, his gaze meeting Brad's challengingly.

Sam was not really surprised to discover that their rooms were directly across the hall from each other.

It was just one more grotesque irony on this ill-omened day.

Brad unlocked the door and Sam entered. She glanced around nervously. "What a beautiful room. The furniture is nicer than what I have at my apartment—"

"Sam..."

"Why, look, you can see the ocean!"

"Sam..."

"And what a nice big TV. Let's see what's on—"

"Sam, we are *not* going to watch TV."

Sam looked at his grim face, and unconsciously her hand crept to her throat. "We're not?" she squeaked.

"No, we're not. You're going to tell me who the hell the father of your baby is." He loomed over her. "That damned Frenchman?"

"Jean-Paul?" she repeated stupidly.

He turned away, yanking at his tie, loosening the knot, and began pacing around the room. "No, it couldn't be him. Jeanette told me you broke up with him right after Christmas. So who is it? Some new guy? Some old boyfriend? I never would have believed you would be so careless, such a fool as to let some jerk take advantage of you. He must have been a real smooth operator to get past your guard. Are you in love with him? Tell me who he is. Just his name..." He put his balled fist against the palm of his other hand.

Sam's bouquet slipped from her fingers. "Brad! Are you crazy? I'm not pregnant!"

He stopped pacing. "You're not..." His eyebrows went up, then down, then down farther. "We need to talk," he said ominously.

Sam stared up into familiar gray-blue eyes. She

didn't want to talk. If they talked, she would have to tell him the truth—that she'd lied to prevent him from marrying Heather. And if she told him that, he would probably be even more furious than he already was. So furious that he might leave her before she had a chance to convince him that he would be much, much happier with her than he ever would have been with Heather.

She needed to convince him—fast.

"Kiss me," she said.

"What?" He looked at her as if she'd gone insane. And maybe she had.

"Kiss me," she repeated.

He hesitated. "Sam, I don't know if that's a good idea...."

"Oh, for heaven's sake!" she burst out. She threw her arms around his neck and kissed him with all the pent-up passion she'd been suppressing for the past three days—or was it for the past three years?

Automatically, his arms came around her. She slid her hands up into his hair and pressed herself against him.

She heard him draw in a sharp breath. Then suddenly, *he* was kissing *her,* his hands sliding down to pull her hips more closely to him.

She was lost in the thrill of his kiss. The champagne she'd drunk earlier had tasted flat, but now she felt the bubbles in her blood, making her dizzy and giddy. Dear heaven, how she wanted this. How she wanted *him*—

He lifted his mouth from hers. "Sammy...we must talk...ah, dear God, you taste so sweet, you would tempt a damn saint—"

Thump! Thump! Thump!

The sudden pounding on the door startled them both. Breathing heavily, Brad let go of her and ran his fingers through his hair. "Who the hell could that be?" he muttered.

"I have no idea." Whoever it was, she wished they would go away. She wanted Brad to kiss her again....

Thump! Thump! Thump!

With an exasperated sigh, Brad strode to the door and opened it.

Joel and a red-faced Heather stood on the threshold.

Joel, his hand clamped around Heather's wrist, dragged her into the room. Ignoring Brad, he said to Sam, "Has he told you?"

Sam frowned in confusion. "Told me what?"

"Oh, hell," Brad muttered.

Sam glanced at him then back at Joel. "Told me what?" she repeated.

"That you're not really married. That the minister was a fake."

"What!"

Joel nodded grimly. "As fake as the engagement between Heather and Rivers." He glared at Brad. "I'll let you explain the rest. Heather and I have some important business to attend to."

Heather roused from her sullen stance. "What are you talking about? I'd say our business is completely finished."

Joel smiled grimly. "We're taking the red-eye to Las Vegas. This time when we get married, it will be legal."

"Why, you big ape, I wouldn't marry you..."

Sam stared at the door that slammed closed behind them, muffling the rest of Heather's insult.

Then slowly, she turned to look at Brad.

Chapter Thirteen

Brad rubbed the back of his neck. "I was going to tell you...."

"Were you? What, exactly, were you going to tell me?"

"Everything...dammit, stop looking at me like that. You were the one who launched yourself at me like a sex-starved lunatic when I said we needed to talk."

Sam's face felt hotter than a second-degree sunburn. "I didn't know then that everything you've told me for the last three weeks has been a *lie*." She closed her eyes for a moment, remembering the agony of the last several weeks as she tried to prevent him from marrying Heather. "You weren't really engaged?"

"No. Heather is an actress. I paid her to play the part of my fiancée."

Sam stared at him. "Why? *Why* would you do such a thing?"

He ran his fingers through his hair. "Because I was at my wits' end trying to figure out how to get you to see me as something besides a friend! I knew it was a long shot, but I thought seeing me engaged to a gorgeous blonde might wake you up." A ghost of a smile curved his mouth. "If that failed, I hoped you might sacrifice yourself to save me from Heather's clutches—I figured you would never allow me to marry someone as bitchy as she pretended to be."

"Pretended...you mean that was all an act?" Sam's hands clenched. "All those remarks about taking you for your money and hating children?"

A gleam lit his eyes. "Well, you've always been so protective of me. I knew you'd never let her get away with it."

She glared at him. He knew her too well! "You invited five hundred people to a fake wedding?"

"It got a little out of hand. Heather thought it would be out of character for her to plan a small wedding. And she thought your sister could use the business."

Sam bit her lip. Jeanette *had* appreciated the business. But did he have to make Heather sound so considerate? "What about that stupid rat charity? Was that all fake, too?"

He nodded. "I knew it was a little over the top, but I thought for sure you wouldn't let me marry anyone who was trying to save rats."

Sam glared at him. "What about that night at the shop? Did you know I was trying to get you to kiss me?"

"Not exactly. I knew something was going on when Heather told me Kristin had asked her to go to the shop at 10:30 p.m. to look over the menus, but I didn't know what until I arrived and you were, er, so *friendly.*"

"You…" Sam raised her fist, trying to think of a name bad enough to call him. "You *Hollywood tree rat!*"

He caught her wrist easily. "Come on, Sam, look at it from my side. Do you know what it was like for me when you asked me to kiss you? Do you know how long I've waited to hear those words from you? Do you know how afraid I was that I wouldn't be able to stop once I started?"

Warmth swirled up inside her, but she repressed it ruthlessly, crossing her arms over her chest. "You lied to me," she said stonily.

His eyebrows rose. "If we're going to talk about lies—you said you were pregnant."

Heat crept up into her cheeks. "That was different. I didn't realize you would believe I was really pregnant. I was just trying to stop you from marrying Heather."

"You're about as consistent as a weathervane. After Heather had lunch with you, she told me she was sure you were in love with me—but when I came to your apartment last night you acted as if you wanted me to marry her. You insisted that I marry her."

Sam's cheeks burned hotter. "I heard Joel and Heather arguing in the parking lot. He said she was pregnant. I thought the baby was yours."

Brad's brow cleared. "I see. So you decided to martyr yourself." He glanced skyward. "I must be crazy. You're going to drive me insane."

"Me!" Sam lifted her chin, although her heart was beating double-time. "What about you? Was this elaborate charade really necessary?"

"I don't know." He took her hands in his, his gaze serious. "Nothing else I'd tried worked. And if I heard you say one more time what a 'nice guy' I was, or that I was 'like a brother' to you, I was going to commit violence."

"But you never acted as though you were interested in me. You told me you were in love with Blanche Milken!"

He snorted. "With good reason. I saw the way you backed off at the slightest sexual overture. You kept all your boyfriends at arm's length. The first time they pressed you for any kind of commitment, you dumped them faster than a load of garbage. The only way I could have any kind of relationship with you was to pretend I had no more interest in you than a brother."

"That's not true," she said weakly.

"It *was* true. Furious as I was when you brought that damned Frenchman to Christmas—after being gone two whole years!—I knew you would dump him soon enough."

"I'm surprised you didn't give up on me."

"I almost did a couple of times. I tried dating other women, but I knew I would never care about anyone the way I cared about you. No matter how frustrated you made me."

She stared down at the dried bits of grass on her pink lace shoes. "You make me sound horrible."

"No. You weren't. I knew how upset you were when your father left your mother. I saw how Jeanette's pregnancy and quick marriage affected you. It would have been surprising if you weren't a little wary of men."

Her vision blurred. Somehow, he had always understood her. Even when she hadn't understood herself. How had she ever survived without him?

"I wish you'd said something sooner," she said. "Oh, you were probably right about how I would have reacted, but maybe not. I can't read your mind, Brad. You're going to have to tell me what you're feeling."

His hands tightened on hers. "It isn't easy for me to talk about something when I care a great deal." He took a deep breath and looked down into her eyes, his gaze serious and intent. "I love you, Sam. I always have. So much so that it hurts. But I can't wait for you any longer. You're going to have to make up your mind right now. Do you love me or not?"

Tears filled her eyes. "Of course I love you. I was an idiot not to have realized it before."

The blue of his eyes grew more intense than ever. And then he kissed her until she was laughing and breathless.

"Marry me," he murmured in her ear. "For real this time."

She nodded happily, then put her fingers up to his mouth when he leaned forward to kiss her again. "I do have a few conditions, though."

She felt him tense. "Oh?"

"You must teach me to in-line skate...."

The tension eased out of his shoulders. A smile curved his mouth. "I can *try* to teach you. I'm not making any promises. What else?"

"You don't support any more rat charities...."

"That can be arranged. Anything else?"

"You help me out of this perfectly hideous dress."

His eyes gleamed. He pulled the pink zipper down the length of her back. ''Sammy, your wish is my command.''

* * * * *

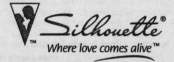

If you enjoyed what you just read,
then we've got an offer you can't resist!

Take 2 bestselling love stories FREE!

Plus get a FREE surprise gift!

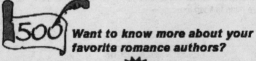

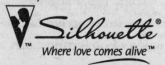

SILHOUETTE *Romance*

COMING NEXT MONTH

SRCNM0703